The Curse of *Bêti*

SITA SEECHARRUN HARRIS

This edition was published by
Shakra Publishers Bristol, U.K.

ISBN 9798815745667

We shall forever remember those

who built the steps we tread upon

For each blade of grass and

each drop of sweat this island knew

at its infancy in development.

We are grateful to our forefathers

to have built

where we live and love now.

Dedication

For my Mum who would have been happy and proud to see this book, as she always wanted me to write. Love you Ma.

For my husband whose love and support were next to the confidence in me to write. His trust in my ability to do so is priceless.

For Mr Beekrumsingh Ramlallah who took a personal initiative to gather and bid to run the preservation of the site where the first indentured labourers disembarked in Mauritius. A historic site since 1985, the Coolie Ghat at Immigration Square, in Port Louis was thus renamed as Aapravasi Ghat, officially inaugurated by the late Indian Prime Minister Indira Gandhi in 1970. Mr Ramlallah used his private funds and with the help of volunteers to clear rubble off the site and save thousands of badly kept records going into the doldrums.

In 1976 most of the rescued records were finally moved to the Mahatma Gandhi Archives after being housed in a private building. From then on, the public had access to search their ancestry and roots back to India. With the privileged bilateral relations between India and Mauritius, people who can retrace their origins in India can apply for an OCI (Overseas Citizen of India) card.

Today, Aapravasi Ghat, in Mauritius, sits proudly in the books of the first UNESCO World Heritage Site due to the tremendous efforts to bring to recognition the tiny island's contribution on the world stage by its unique human history.

In 1998, Beekrumsingh Ramlallah funded and erected a bust of Adolphe de Plevitz who was, to him, the greatest champion of these indentured labourers. Without doubt his indomitable spirit of fighting for both individual and collective dignity and self-respect, and to get one's place in the sun, that led him to take up the larger national cause when the times demanded it, as the shackles of colonialism began to loosen.

In 1942, after his release from the army Beekrumsingh Ramlallah founded a voluntary (non-military) brigade named Mauritius Sewa Samiti. The aim of that brigade was to serve the under-privileged and the suffering masses and to inculcate the spirit of service, self-help, self-reliance and good breeding among them. This institution was the first of many that he subsequently built or helped to set up and/or develop. Collectively, they represent his lasting legacy to this country in fields as diverse as social work, religion, culture, education, health, governance, politics and journalism. His aim was to ensure social justice for all and to restore the dignity of the common man, especially the downtrodden. This meant confronting a system with feudal undertones which was firmly anchored in the quasi-divine belief that a privileged few were born to forever lord it over others: some were born to rule, others were meant to be dominated.

To combat entrenched reflexes and attitudes in both the rulers and the ruled and bring about the much-needed change and transformation, the only solution was to create awareness and mobilise the people, but also to lead by example.

In 1956, with the cooperation of a friend, Premchand Dabee, he led a Mauritius-wide campaign to convince the British government that one of its top priorities should be the education of children, especially of those who could not afford private schooling. The campaign 'Admit our Children' was a great success. He also organised the 'Down with Proportional Representation' campaign and opposed the demand for a quota system for the majority community, insisting that the only criterion should be meritocracy. As far back as 1946, to popularise books and magazines on socialism (which was then taboo in Mauritius), literature and magazines of Indian interest (in English and Hindi), he founded the Nalanda Bookshop. A few years later he founded the Nalanda Press Service to give an opportunity to those who wanted to publish pamphlets and booklets on socialism and in Hindi.

Mr Beekrumsingh Ramlallah has left his imprint on many other organizations such as the Small Scale Industries Board; the Police and Local Government Service Commissions; the State Bank; the Health Education Division of the Ministry of Health; the Mauritius Peace Council; the Mauritius Family Planning Association; the Mauritius Housing Corporation; the Ex-Servicemen Welfare Fund Committee; the Mauritius Government Tourist and the Tea Advisory Boards; the Court of the University of Mauritius; a Hindi newspaper Nav Jeevan which he founded in 1960 with Mungur Bhagat; the Hindu Maha Sabha and the Sanatana Dharma Temples Federation; the Aapravasi Ghat; the Mauritius Union of Journalists.

However, it is the Mauritius Times which is perhaps his most visible legacy. Founded in 1954, it remains a weekly newspaper which is published in Mauritius, primarily in the English language. It was with great affection that I remember the frail looking bespectacled man whom I called Chacha (Uncle) whenever I visited my dear friend Sadhna Ramlallah at their house in Wellington street, Port Louis. He was a humble, kind and an affable man, but under this persona was a roaring lion who claimed his might under the sun for the downtrodden and all alike.

The memory of each of us today walking in freedom with dignity. bears a great nod of respect to his relentless pursuit of serving his people with utter integrity and selflessness.

For my dear friend and respected true intellectual I have come across, Dr Mrs Sarita Boodhoo, affectionately called Didi. A pure gem by her own social and literary achievements, she remains Mauritius's voice as a resonant post-colonial on the world stage with pride for the Bhojpuri speakers. The majority of Indentured

Indian Girmityas hailed from the Indo Gangetic Hindu belt where Bhojpuri and related Awadh languages are spoken.

She is the Chairperson of Bhojpuri Speaking Union, Founder Director of Mauritius Bhojpuri Institute, a writer, professionally trained journalist, Indologist par excellence and staunch cultural activist since 1956. She set up the World Hindi Secretariat and was Editor in Chief of Jan Vani.

A living national treasure, worthy of recognition for protecting the old Mauritian intangible cultural heritage and keeping it alive.

For every single Mauritian who carries the legacy of our ancestors, who built this rainbow nation. The deliberate extension of a nation's power and influence over other peoples and lands, including the use of territorial seizure, legal justifications for occupation, regimes of racialization, labour exploitation, and forced assimilation. Such dynamics become the conditions from which more indirect forms of rule, military action, and economic control can be established. Such endeavours are incrusted in our island's history and we have to avert its side effects to the best of our abilities as a young nation.

May each of us thrive and live in peace and harmony.

This is the story of people nearly forgotten and unnamed in the history of Mauritius.

The story of slavery, the story of indentured labour, joined in pain of a time none of us alive today have witnessed. Facts twisted by politicians, lobbyists and all those who needed to become a king in their own tower to preside and rule over the mass. Today, the sentiment between the original builders of this country, both slaves and indentured immigrants have been twisted in mistrust, and ethnic division. Despite the fact that each one of us coloured and Mulato Mauritians have had our blood mixed and given generations of mixed bloods.

For, once there was love.

Once, the voices of the workers were one against the master. Today, the clamour is instead lost and buried. It is a sad fact that although some of the indentured descendants can today retrace their family and place of origin, those of the slaves cannot do so. It's a damning truth that many were ripped from their tribal names and were just numbers in a shipload considered as commodities. Once on the sugar estates, they were given objects' names to the fancy of the Commander or scribe. Later on, they were baptised, and some took Christian names. Their identity and mother tongues were totally wiped by force.

Although this is a work of fiction, I have drawn strongly on historical record and fact to recreate the period of Indian indenture on the island of Mauritius which was colonised by both the French and the British.

whoever utters it, regardless of their race.

My feelings about it are rooted in my walks to school, interacting with other fellow students in my class, displaying their ethnicity, remnants of slavery, indenture, and of both fused culturally and genetically through intermarriage.

The Whites, as ruling class however, remained distanced from the working class. Even their schools remained private, exclusive, and they chose their language of instruction to be 'French' as per the legitimate inheritance of their forefathers, the rulers and masters of the island. In the course of folding history into this story, I have taken some liberties, changing the names of key players, and fictionalising certain geographic locations, heredity, religious practices and rituals, folklore, cultures and languages, sugar estates, plantations, among others, on which the indentured workers and former slaves lived. There has not been any intention to offend, but to reproduce a sense of the racialised hierarchies and brutality of the time based upon written records and publications.

Those who love us, never leave us alone with our grief. At the moment they show us our wound, they reveal they have the medicine.

I'm not sure there was ever a harder read than this, for those of us duty bound to carry the ancestors, to work for them, as we engage in daily life in different parts of the world where they were brought in chains. Where they, as slaves to cruel, or curious, or indifferent, white persons (with few exceptions) existed in precarious suspension disconnected from their real life, and where we also have had to struggle to protect our humanity, to experience joy of life, in spite of everything evil we have witnessed or to which we have been subjected.

We should not be struck with the realization that it is like naming something we ourselves work hard to avoid, how lonely we are too, in foreign lands we have migrated to, intentionally or by accident: it has been lonely for our true culture, our people, our singular connection to a specific understanding of the world we grew up into.

 We see something else: the nobility of a soul that has suffered to the point almost of erasure, and still it struggles to be whole, present, giving. Growing in love, deepening in understanding. Offering peace. Here is the medicine: that though the heart is breaking, happiness can exist in a moment, also. Due to the moment in which we live all the time there really is, we can keep going. It may be true, and often is, that every person we hold dear is taken from us at some point.

Still. From moment to moment, we drive to carry on as if nothing ever happened, we watch our beans and our watermelons grow. We plant. We hope. We harvest. We share with neighbours. Life, inexhaustible, goes on. We do too.

Carrying our wounds and our medicines, as we go.

शकर – Sugar

The etymology of sugarcane dates back to the Pre-Aryan period of the Indus Valley civilization, around 5000 BC.

Vessels boiling sugarcane have been found in the excavations. As of late 13 BCE, sugre, from Old French sucre "sugar" stems from Medieval Latin succarum, from Arabic al-sukkar, from Persian shakar, from Sanskrit sharkara "ground or candied sugar," originally "grit, gravel" (cognate with Greek kroke "pebbles").

The Arabic word, also, was borrowed in Italian (zucchero), Spanish azùcar during the Moorish empire in Andalusia, and German (Old High German zucura, German Zucker), and its forms are represented in most European languages (such as Serbian cukar, Polish cukier, Russian sakhar).

Its OldWorld home was India (Alexander the Great's companions marvelled at the "honey without bees") and it remained exotic in Europe until the Arabs began to cultivate it in Sicily and Spain. Not until after the Crusades did it begin to rival honey as the West's sweetener. The Spaniards in the West Indies began raising sugar cane in 1506; first grown in Cuba 1523; first cultivated in Brazil 1532.

The first chemically refined sugar appeared on the scene in India about 2,500 years ago (Indus/Harappa). Trade existed between the sandy deserts and fertile banks of Egypt and Indus valleys. The hieroglyphs found on the walls of the kings depict sugarcane as part of the great fortunes entombed for the emperors' afterlife.

Sugar making techniques spread east towards China, and west towards Persia and the early Islamic worlds, eventually reaching the Mediterranean in the 13th century. Cyprus and Sicily became important centres for sugar production. Throughout the Middle Ages, it was considered a rare and expensive spice, rather than an everyday condiment. The first written reference to sugar occurs in 325 B.C. after the conquest of Persia and the attempted invasion of India by Alexander the Great. One of his admirals, Niarchos, while sailing down the Indus river, wrote to his amazement, "a reed in India that brings forth honey without the help of bees." Perhaps this reference to honey indicates not simply the sweetness of the newfound sugar but also to its colour – that the Indians had not yet developed the process of creating clear white crystals. He also noted the Indians consumed a pudding made of rice, milk, sugar, and cardamom, what today we might call a 'sweet rice', commonly known as kheer in India. The Greeks referred to rice as Oryza which linguists believe to be a loan word from Tamil 'arici' meaning rice. Alexander brought these items back and spread them throughout his empire. Today, the small oblong shaped pasta 'Orzo' still exists linking it to what the Greek shaped as rice from what was introduced to them by Alexander the Great.

A brief timeline:

- 350BC Indians discovered how to crystallize sugar during the Gupta dynasty.

- 600 AD Sugar reaches Persia and the Mediterranean.

- In 1652 Jan van Riebeek founded the Dutch Cape Colony (now Cape Town).

- 1820 British settlers arrived in South Africa.

- 1834 Slavery is abolished across the British Empire.

- 1834 Thirty-six indentured coolies arrived in Mauritius aboard the Atlas.

- 1847 Edmund Marwood grew sugarcane in South Africa for the first time.

- 1856 British Parliament passes the Indenture Bill.

- 1859 The ship Shah Alum to Mauritius sinks. Only one of 400 indentured coolies survive while all the seventy-five crew members are rescued.

The taste for sweetness in food and drink is universal, and the cultivation of sugar is global. A great variety of sugarcane is cultivated in the tropics, while sugar beet is cultivated in temperate regions. However, the engine behind the rise of sugar's popularity was cane sugar. Its early history, in Indonesia, India and China, was small-scale and aimed solely at local markets.

When sugar cane was transplanted to plantations in the Mediterranean, then into islands in the Atlantic, the story changed – and even more dramatically, when sugar crossed the Atlantic to the Americas. There, sugar cane was cultivated and converted to sugar by enslaved Africans (themselves shipped across the Atlantic). It was this slave-grown sugar that brought about revolutionary changes in the landscape of the sugar colonies while transforming the tastes of the Western world. As Europeans and Americans settled and traded with the wider world in the course of the nineteenth century, they transplanted commercial sugar cultivation to new locations: to islands in the Indian Ocean, to Africa, Indonesia, to Pacific islands and to Australia. Wherever sugar took hold, local sugar planters had difficulties with labour. They found the answer in imported, slaves and indentured labour. From one sugar region to another – from Brazil to Hawaii – the sugar plantation became the home of alien people – people who had been uprooted and shipped vast distances to undertake the gruelling, intensive labour on sugar plantations. For all that, sugar plantations more than proved their worth to their owners and investors. But there was a price to pay for the development of the sugar plantation. The natural environments were hugely damaged by the development of sugar. From Barbados in the 1640s to the Florida Everglades in recent years, the ecological harm caused by sugar plantations has been enormous and is only now being fully recognized. It is, however, the human cost of sugar cultivation which is most obvious and dramatic. It is at its most visible in the labour force, from the first slave gangs in sixteenth-century Brazil through to indentured Indian labourers in Fiji, the Japanese in Hawaii or the 'South Sea Islanders' shipped to Australia in the late nineteenth century.

Cultivating sugar cane was a harsh business, and it was the labour of slaves and indentured labourers that transformed sugar from a luxury item to an essential commodity. Within the space of two centuries – roughly between 1700 and 1900 – sugar became a dietary essential for all sorts of people the world over.

From the earliest days of slave-grown sugar in the Americas, sugar was so important, so central, that it became a source of political, economic and international dispute. Even today, sugar is a topic of intense discussion between nations and within international organisations. It serves to create a confusing welter of interests, commodities and prices, all of them weaving together the various producers and consumers, different international organisations and diverse agreements into a global web spun by the world's need for sugar. In many respects, sugar has been bad for centuries; it was bad for its labour force (slaves and indentured labourers), and it was bad for the ecology of sugar-growing regions.

Now we learn that sugar is the prime cause of mounting ill health among nations all over the world. Nonetheless, sugar continues to be consumed in enormous volumes by more and more people. Sugar remains popular – more popular, in quantitative terms, than ever before. Sugar has pulled, displaced, bullied, abused, enslaved people, created new ruling classes, pedantry, geopolitical conflicts, erased native cultures and damaged generations.

We know that sugar cane entered the world of Islam from India. Buddhist cuisine in India had adopted sugar as a basic ingredient as early as 260 BC and, in time, sugar began to influence the cuisine of greatly diverse societies across South-East Asia. Sugar also moved slowly westward from India into Africa, the Middle East and the Mediterranean. As Islam spread, so too did the cultivation and consumption of sugar cane. By 1400, it was being cultivated in Egypt, Syria, Jordan, North Africa, Spain and possibly Ethiopia and Zanzibar.

Sugar was on the move – in all directions.

In 1258, following the fall of Baghdad to the Mongols, elements of local cuisine began a protracted movement eastward to China and to Asiatic Russia. Indeed, this global transfer was to be a feature of sugar – it was part of imperial expansion. Major empires – Greek, Roman, Islamic, Mongol, Byzantine, Ottoman and European – all absorbed foodstuffs and cuisines inherited from older empires, states and conquered peoples. All placed great value on the sweetening powers of honey and, increasingly, of cane sugar.

Sugar thus became one of the unrecognized bounties of imperial conquest and power, seized and absorbed by conquerors then carried to distant corners of the globe where it shaped new tastes and a demand for the pleasure it brought. In the European context, it was also to bring unimaginable profit. The British Empire with the creation of the East India Company bears testimony to that rise of wealth for the British crown.

By around 1600, sugar had undergone a remarkable transformation. What had, up to this point, been the preserve of the rich and powerful, was now available in the humblest of shops and in the smallest of villages. It had begun to change from an expensive luxury to the everyday necessity of ordinary people. Even more curious is the fact that this massive change in direction and fortunes was all made possible by the brutal exploitation of vast numbers of African slaves and indentured workers from the colonies.

How the Indian Ocean Was Made?

Until about 100 years ago, people believed that the oceans and continents were fixed in place. In 1912, a geologist named Alfred Wegener came up with a theory in a book called The Origin of Continents and Oceans. Wegener argued that the seven continents that exist today had all been part of one giant land mass, a supercontinent called Pangaea. This supercontinent had begun to break up into pieces, with the pieces then gradually drifting apart from each other and into the positions they occupy today. Wegener was not the first to come up with an idea like this. Since the sixteenth century, cartographers and geologists had been puzzled by the fact that the continents seemed to fit together, like the pieces of a jigsaw puzzle. Could they have once been joined together? We now know that Wegener was on the right track. Various land masses did come together to form a massive supercontinent about 270 million years ago. Take a look at the map of Pangaea and you'll see that India, Australia, Madagascar,

Antarctica and Africa were all stuck to each other—and that the Indian Ocean didn't even exist then. About 175 million years ago, Pangaea began to break apart due to plate tectonics. It first broke into two large pieces called Laurasia and Gondwana. The land masses that we know today as North America, Europe and Asia were part of Laurasia, while Gondwana was made up of South America, Africa, Australia, India and Antarctica. Eventually, Laurasia and Gondwana broke up into even smaller pieces. India and Madagascar probably broke away from Africa about 160 million years ago and broke away from Antarctica and Australia about 130 million years ago. About 90 million years ago, India broke away from Madagascar and began drifting north.

Between 85 and 45 million years ago, Australia and Antarctica separated, and the Australian plate moved north to fuse with the Indian plate, creating the Indo-Australian plate.

As it drifted north, the Indo-Australian plate collided with something in its way: the Eurasian plate. The force of the collision pushed the land upwards, creating the Himalayas. The land that was pushed upwards to create the Himalayas was once under the gigantic Tethys Sea, which encircled Pangaea. In fact, the fossils of sea creatures that were discovered on top of the mountains provided proof of plate tectonics, which is the idea that the Earth's crust is made up of many pieces, or plates, that continue to move very (very) slowly.

The Indian plate has continued to push against the Eurasian plate ever since, which is why the Himalayas are growing taller by about 5 mm every year. Earthquakes are common in the area because of the force exerted by the plates pushing against each other. This is also true of other places in the world where the boundaries of plates push against each other.

In fact, the fault line between the Indo-Australian plate and the Sunda plate (the plate that most of South-east Asia is on) is where the epicentre of the December 2004 earthquake occurred.

The Indian Ocean thus came into being when water rushed in to occupy the space between land masses that were once joined together. The description above is quite a simplified version of the sequence of events that created the Indian Ocean, while the story isn't over, yet.

The plates of the Earth continue to move, which means the Indian Ocean and the lands bordering it continue to shift and change. Two more undersea earthquakes occurred away from the main fault line (between the Indo-Australian and Sunda plates) in April 2012.

This has made seismologists who study earthquakes think that the Indian and Australian plates are now separating. That could bring more earthquakes and tsunamis to the Indian Ocean region in the future. There are other things that are changing in the Indian Ocean too. The coastlines that we are familiar with didn't always look the way they do now. The sea level has changed over the years due to the warming and cooling of our planet. Since the last Ice Age, which occurred 18–20,000 years ago, the sea level has risen by 120 metres as the ice sheets have melted. This melting and the subsequent flooding of the coastlines have had a major impact on the history of our early ancestors. The shifting of sand and silt by rivers and, of course, human activity, have also had an impact on the Indian Ocean landscape.

Bêti - Hindi Word बेटि meaning Daughter

Beti people - a Central African ethnic group

Beti language - a group of Bantu languages in Central and West Africa

Beti language (Côte d'Ivoire) or Eotile, a nearly extinct Tano language

Chapter 1

तापू - Country

I was born by the sea.

This place. This place, Bêti thought, as she looked across the bay, was in her bones. From here, Port Louis had not changed. She walked along this path for more years than she cared to remember. It grew ever more breath-taking. Far out across the land, beyond the winding river du Pouce, she could see the emerald glitter of the sea and beyond, she could make out the shadow of the harbour's rugged coastline with the oil silos and the Baie du Tombeau winding away in the far north.

Bêti imagined that beneath the scrubby banks, shining black basalt pebbles washed by the shores in the low evening sun and in the depths of water, she fancied a lifetime of memories. So many of them played out against these riverbanks bordered by bridge walls, within the belly of the city. She could almost hear this famous creole lullaby being hummed softly, which talks of a conversation between and old lady and a young boy about how she is managing her life amidst her poverty, while she replies that she is fishing some chubs for a meal:

'*Mo passé la rivière Tanier, mo zouène ène grand mama, mo dire li ki li fer la? Li dire li la pêss cabots mo Piti. Couma ou a pé debriyé*
Mo dir li avec mo douler
Mo pé tal la main pou gagne mo la vie'

*

I went by the Lataniers River
I met an old grandma.
I asked her what she was doing there,
She said she was fishing chubs.
Alas, alas, my children,
One must work to earn one's living,
Alas, alas, my children,
One must work to earn one's living.

Today, the air murmured into a timely heartbeat of the water's current. It whispered a familiar chant. It always calmed her, walking along the river's edge. Sometimes, it was hard to believe that so many decades had passed since she'd spent her summers along this sunny path.

Today, as always, it was exhilarating in its freshness, a landscape forever shifting yet its fabric remained the same, for all time. The straw-green flanks of Signal mountain from where the city started, were surely smaller than in her childhood, as though the weight of time had obliged them to crouch just a little lower with each passing year.

It was perhaps the way islands morph our perceptions, she thought. Making everything small and reachable. What was this tiny island to her, lost in the vast ocean? No doubt everything yet nothing at all.

An island in the subtropical Capricorn; a result of a huge huffing and puffing of the earth's crust resulting in a plateau riddled with volcanoes. When all the lava work had finished, her island was born out of the vast expanse of the Indian Ocean. It stood as a lone rock surrounded by the clearest and most stunning lagoons of the world.

Her fascination with the sea stems probably from the fact that is all she knew and could see in her daily life when she grew up.

Why was this extensive body of shimmering water in all shades and hues of blues so mesmerising? Perhaps it is the lack of knowledge of what lies beneath the surface, or just appeared as a place of mystery.

People standing on shore can see only as far as the horizon, and until comparatively recently, had no means of knowing what lay beyond. She recalled fables of seamen, ships' voyages, sea monsters and distant shores. Lands where they met strangers who spoke in different tongues unheard of, and brought new knowledge, lore and cultures to these seafarers. Her closest account of them were in the nursery rhymes and colourfully illustrated books at the junior library of the capital.

Like her favourite one which she sang nonstop until her throat got parched.

*'Il était un petit navire, il était un petit navire, qui n'avait
ja-jamais-jamais navigué, qui n'avait ja-jamais navigué,
Oé Oé matelot!'*

No doubt the seamen grumbled and swore, for that is
the way at sea.
Life was never easy on board a ship, at the mercy of
the elements. The fishermen's handmade boats looked
like little toys playing toss and tumble with the waves
next to the ships built to last longer.

It is night and the moon sit low and glowing upon the
water.
The sky does not shy away from displaying its coat of
shining stars, so clear that she thought she could just
stretch her arm and catch one.

It is this quality of her island's sky, sea and lushness
that made her fall in love again and again with her
country drilling into her soul.

इंसान - Humans

In the making of connections between human societies, the role of the sea is particularly fascinating. Connections across large open spaces have brought together peoples, religions and civilizations in stimulating ways. Sometimes this has been through individual encounters, as travellers, including pilgrims and merchants, finding themselves visiting alien environments; sometimes it has been the result of mass migrations that have changed the character of regions. Sometimes, it has been the result as much of the movement of goods as of people, when the inhabitants of distant lands saw, admired, and sold over wealth which could be made on distant shores.

It was such a promise that was made to the biggest wave of immigrants who boarded the ships in Calcutta to my island under the gleefully greedy British India officers. Indentured workers were lured into stories of finding gold under boulders covering the island. When you speak of gold to an Indian, it sparkles faster in his mind than fresh air. As we say in the local jargon 'couma dire diable fine trouve camphre'* So, they came, toiled under the tropical sun, moved huge rocks but never found any gold. However, they discovered that they were not able to return back to their country, out of bondage from the masters who 'owned' them. Yet they stayed, lived, produced children and settled down on this land which later would explode in prosperity and be called 'paradise'.

They also loved the sea which had become their main umbilical cord between their distant homes and the new ones they made. This sea was beautiful, and mesmerising. Its colours shone like none they had seen where they originally came from, where murkiness was the trademark. Here, it changed its colours into a myriad of clean blue tones depending

---

* couma dire diable fine trouve camphre – like the devil which has found camphor. A popular statement in Creole in Mauritius.

upon how clear the cerulean sky above was, while the breeze remained pleasant.

A look at a map reveals a fundamental difference between the other Oceans and the Indian Ocean. The shores of the Indian Ocean made it into a network of traders. Remote, widely scattered islands such as Mauritius and Réunion were discovered and settled by Europeans and those they brought with them as slaves or indentured servants. The Indian Ocean is hard to measure. To say it covers 75,000,000 square kilometres or 27 per cent of the world's maritime space is to assume we know where its arbitrarily drawn southern limit should lie. The voyage that my ancestors made across the Indian Ocean could have started earlier when the Portuguese entered the Indian Ocean in 1497, the Cape of Good Hope, giving access to the Atlantic. They came to my island, found water, caught and ate the flightless Dodos who had never seen any humans before and trusted these huge two-legged upright animals. Sadly, they all finished into a pile of bones, spat after a dinner made of their fleshy bodies. Until, not one was ever seen running under the canopies of the tambalacoque*. History was made, the Dodo became the most popular example of a species made extinct by humans.

It seems odd to speak of 'the slow creation' of the Indian Ocean, as if this space had not been in existence for millions of years before sea traffic began to pass along its shores and across its open spaces.

But from the perspective of maritime history the question is when the Indian Ocean began to function as a unit. In other words, when the coasts of east Africa, Arabia, India and south-east Asia began to interact across the sea, whether through migration or through trade. In addition to breaking down these shores into a series of discrete, and at times quite disconnected, coasts, attention has to focus on the two major gulfs that penetrate deep into the Middle East, the Red Sea and the Persian Gulf, channels that gave access to two of the earliest, richest and most

---

* tambalacoque – endemic tree to Mauritius

innovative civilizations of the ancient world, those of ancient Egypt and Mesopotamia.

To say that they made very profitable use of the sea routes running south-eastwards would be an understatement. As we know, far too well how the East India company displaced, and quelled the mighty Spaniards, the ace Arab Seafarers, the astute Portuguese and the explorative French to forge the biggest empire the world had seen with riches extending to spices, sugar, gold, tea and silk at unprecedented scales.

My ancestors didn't know the whips on their backs unlike the African slaves, but their miseries were not less for that reason. They sweated and toiled to make a success of a crop they knew and grew very well in their native homelands. Sugar. It had become the new commodity which rivalled regular voyages which took place around Arabia, linking Egyptian ports on the Red Sea to the Persian Gulf. With produce of the lands along the shores of the Indian Ocean: expensive necessities such as copper, luxury materials such as black ebony and white ivory, as well as aromatic resins such as frankincense and myrrh. Sugar was the new obsession of the rich who never shied away from displaying it in their sumptuous feasts.

Behind clearing the land to grow sugar, the indentured* labourers discovered a prison without walls or bars or boundaries, a prison consisting of infinite skies and endless green fields surrounded by stunning beaches.

There were no ships to take them back from where they came from; but would they really want to go back?

Their masters kept a keen eye upon their possessions and saw to it that the land grew greener with more expanse of sugarcane. The fertile volcanic soil was fine, with excellent drainage, and making the trenches to plant the ratoons (baby canes) was easier than in their homeland where terrible droughts parched the soil. When water from the irrigation canals was let into the fields; the planting, the manuring, the de-weeding carried by both the coolie men, alongside the women in their bright coloured saris which were often faded on areas where they sat and huddled to eat their roti.

The burning of the cane, during the harvest season, when the air would be filled with the aroma of scalded cane-juice was rich, evocative and some women even wept thinking of their loved ones left behind across the ocean.

All day long from dawn to dusk, swarms of them in their dark bodies moved from line to line in the fields with their machetes, hacking down the giant green-yellow and garnet cane-stalks; blackened by ash and burnt cane-juice, they would carry their bundles of cane on their backs and load the ox-carts waiting on the navigation canals. Then the punts, pulled by beautiful Indian cows and bulls slowly made their way along the gridwork of canals to the factory, perched on the edge of the estate. By sunset, the women would return to the 'camp', a communal housing estate for labourers. They had basic facilities but shared a room with all the members of their family. Many made their evening meals on stoves and firewood was mostly dry sugarcane stalks and stumps. Some roti, dhal, pickles or a vegetable were shared before hitting their mattresses, made of cane straw, for a well needed rest for their aching limbs.

Indentureship or Girmitya in the Indian context was a particular form of contracted labour, which has remained largely absent from public discourse, although it has been an important aspect of complex, global and capitalist economic production systems. It bracketed the period of the Atlantic slave trade and spread African, Chinese, European and Indian populations, among others, across four continents. Its inspiration was an imperial desire for a cheap, agricultural workforce. At the height of the British Empire, indentured labour was used in the production of sugar, cocoa, cotton, rubber and tea.

In South and East Africa, indentured labourers were also involved in mining and the creation of railway networks. The British additionally made agreements with the Netherlands and France which meant that these countries were able to recruit and dispatch to their colonies indentured labourers from British India. In the seventeenth century, white European labourers were taken to both North America and the Caribbean on temporary agreements, termed indentures.

In Virginia, prior to slavery, some African indentured labourers also formed part of the bonded workforce. The many abuses of this type of labour are evident in the earliest historical records of the system. Kidnapping and enticement both played a role in securing indentured labourers in Europe, who arrived in uniformly poor conditions and treatment in the Caribbean. Sugar became the favoured product of the Caribbean plantations. However, plantation owners believed that white workers would not suffice in either numbers or cost due to the labour-intensive nature of its manufacture. As a consequence, these labourers and the system that brought them to the Caribbean were replaced by the brutal enslavement of Africans. Following the abolition of the slave trade in 1807, planters in the Caribbean began to consider the possibility that they might revive the system that had served them two centuries earlier.

In 1811, almost three decades before Indian indenture began, a mass importation of Chinese labourers was being mooted as a substitute for the enslaved African workforce.1 Indenture was not slavery, but it consistently featured aspects of that system, and its nineteenth-century incarnation was famously labelled little more than a reinvention of slavery.

The Merriam-Webster dictionary defines coolie as "an unskilled labourer or porter hired for low or subsistence wages." Most likely, the word coolie is derived from the South Indian Tamil word kuli, which means wages normally associated with work performed by people from a lower caste. The word entered the English language in the 1800s when Britain ruled India and, with the British practice of indenture, spread across the world.

Coolie is a derogatory word and the indenture system dehumanized people with this label. Labourers, especially those from the higher castes who took these jobs, felt humiliated and protested when they were addressed as "coolies," but the drudgery of the farm ruthlessly decimated any semblance of

resistance. Indentured coolies were called by different names in the different colonies: sami in South Africa; girmitiyas* in Fiji and Mauritius; the Gladstone coolies in Trinidad; and, as the workers called themselves, jahaji bhais or "ship brothers."
In fact, all Indians irrespective of their occupation were addressed as coolies or sami in the colonies.

---

* girmitiya: Indian servitude worker

Archives

Bêti turned and tossed, she couldn't sleep. Coming back to her native island meant that years of memories were crashing upon her frail body. She could see the bright face of her mother. She never tired telling her of her story and that of her Mum and grandmother. She repeated the troubled feelings she has always had throughout her life. Why did she move from her Uncle's house to her great Aunt's house? What was the mystery of her own parents? She was told that she became an orphan as a toddler. Her own mother ….

'Who was she? Did she really die in childbirth? Or did she not want her?'

This was the part she had been unable to discover among Maman's papers. There was no paper trail leading to her, no trace of her at all, no mention. My real great grandmother's name had been completely obliterated. Despite all the searches in the archives, there was nothing I could find to give my mother closure. She had no face she could put to her mother nor grandmother who took care of her but sadly passed away. Rumours in the family were hushed that she was a French woman who eloped with an Indian Sirdar. Her family cut ties from her, and her in-laws never really accepted her. Her name was never ushered, out of shame. They remained clouded in mystery for Maman while her deep longing for her maternal mother and grandmother drilled a hole in her soul, sometimes pouring out copious amounts of tears. Nobody could give her any answers nor show her a photo of how her mother looked. Was she tall? Short, fair, dusky, pretty, plain looking? Did her nose look like Maman's? All these thickened the mystery.

Bêti never really paid attention to her Mum's accounts of her family, as they were so repetitive that she stopped having any interest in the lack of novelty. But when her Mum died, something strange happened. She yearned to recall each and every word of what her mother told her. She wanted to know the truth. This ached in her flanks and felt bitter in her mouth.

While there is no question that some migrants were indentured willingly, there is also no doubt that many left their homes without full knowledge of the length of the journey they were undertaking, or how far they were travelling. Coercion, misrepresentation and even kidnapping were all recorded forms of 'recruitment', and the exploitation of the indentured subject continued from embarkation to plantation.

Bêti sought solace in her ignorance. Not knowing how and why her ancestors came to this island was worth every drop of tears she saw her own mother cry from forging an invisible map into her mind, devoid of any images.

For now, she braved the city centre once again on her lone walks along the multitude of small paved alley ways. She held her breath while crossing in between the grand bazaar's meat and fish sections. She coughed as the stench gripped at her throat. In a few hours the smell would be unbearable; strong enough to turn the stomach of a strong Konkan fishmonger. Death smells worse in the tropics. Most things do. She entered the shady-covered, cool, wet market where Alouda* curds and Chinese greens were sold. 'Pillay Best Alouda' the sign read. Yes, she remembers that she has never missed gulping one glass of chilled Alouda 'Nature' meaning vanilla flavoured, since she was 12 years of age. The blob of ice cream floating, clashing with the ice cubes were fighting each other to give her the best brain freeze. It felt refreshing, in the sweltering heat outside. Throngs of colourful pastel pastries eyed her blissful moment, drinking the Alouda beckoning 'come on, get one gâteau Français!' But she resisted the temptation of this sugar overdose and continued on her way. She waded through a motley collection of gawkers, hawkers, housewives and public servants whose bellies flop over their overtight trousers all carrying their grey 'official' envelope from their

---

* alouda – a favourite street food -vanilla milk based chilled drink in Mauritius

respective offices. They jostled and pushed ever closer, while Bêti avoided those who bumped into her with their sweaty bodies. Social distance was an unknown concept to islanders.

An hour later, Bêti stood outside the entrance to number 14 Jardin Lane. It was a dilapidated two-storey building. If there was one thing Port Louis wasn't short of, it was dilapidated buildings. The whole place seemed to consist of these decaying, overcrowded dwellings, which crawled with humanity in their burnished skin under the tropical sun. The building's entrance had, at one time, been painted a cheerful bright blue, but the paint had long ago lost the battle against unrelenting sun and tropical rain. Now only a few pale traces lingered, streaks of watery blue on mould-covered grey-green plaster, a fading testimony to more prosperous times. Above, the remains of a balcony jutted out like broken teeth, its iron railings strutting in bars with pointed arrowheads on timber ceilings ending in white lambrequins strangled by foliage from a nearby mango tree.

Bêti knocked at the door and waited. Sounds. Feet shuffling towards her; then someone fiddling with a padlock. The thin wooden door rattled and finally opened just a crack. A shrivelled old man dressed in a navy peon uniform with a shock of untidy silver hair stood stooped like a question mark in front of Bêti. Tanned skin, parchment thin, hung off his stick-like frame, so that he looked like some fragile caged bird. The old man looked up at Bêti and asked,

"What do you want?"

"Is this the Archives?"

"Yes, indeed, take the stairs and turn to your right."

Unexpectedly, the peon followed Bêti, after closing the door. As if to make sure she was to be trusted. He led the way, shuffling down a long, darkened hallway, the air cool and heavy with the scent of rose incense.

Bêti followed, her heels echoing on the polished floor. The interior was tasteful, almost opulent, and a stark contrast to the building's shabby exterior. The old man stopped at the end of the corridor and ushered her into a large, well-appointed drawing room. The place looked like it used to be the house of a rich Surtee* merchant. But many had left the capital for cooler heights and greener areas instead of a small courtyard that came with such houses. A middle-aged Indian woman entered, the old man following behind her like a subservient faithful pet. Twenty years ago, she'd have been considered a beauty. A full figure, coffee-coloured skin and brown eyes lined with kohl came in from a door on the side. Her hair was parted in the middle and tied tightly in a bun. On her forehead a smudge of vermillion. She wore a neatly pleated sari, with a zari border. Beneath her blouse displayed a bare midriff which came into view every time she moved her arms upwards trying to grab a box of files. Her wrists were adorned with a pair of gold bangles and from her neck hung an ornate gold Mangal sutra studded with small black beads. She was like many Indians in the countryside who gravitated towards a public servant's job for its ease and financial security. She was going to be the agent

---

* surtee – from Surat, Gujurat, India

who could help Bêti find some answers to her queries. Flashing a large bright smile, she nodded in her direction and spoke in a soft voice.

"How can I help you today, Madam? Are you looking to trace back your ancestry?"

Well, in fact most people who visited the Archives had this in mind. Mine was not so straight forward.

"Oh, Hello, yes, indeed, I have come to do that…. but"

She looked at Bêti waiting for the next words to come out, as if she had had a lot of similar drills.

"Well, I am trying to look for my great, great grandmother's identity which seemed to have been omitted on my mother's side. Do you think you can help me find it?"

She moved forward and smiled.

"Yes, I can try, do you have your mother's birth certificate? What was the name of your great grandmother?"

Bêti quickly wrote the name and handed her the papers. After scanning them, she frowned.

"Hmm… that's strange. Why would there be a blank there? Was she adopted?"

"No! Not that I know"

"No worries, I could try that period of dates of the arrival of the indentured immigrants."

"I am convinced", Beti thought.

She knew something out there was lurking to send her doubts into a spiral of mystery.

After rummaging through a lot of boxes with musty smelling files, she found nothing.

There were no records about her mother's maternal lineage.

The sari clad woman was now in sweats and wiping her forehead frequently looking at the clock on the wall.

She was ready for her lunch break. This is something every public servant is very punctual about; the rest can be stretched to how far it needs to go, but the lunch break and time to go home we're sacred rituals. Bêti left the archives and returned to the blazing heat outside.

She took a side alley, and outside felt like a furnace.

It's not for any reason that the Alouda was the most loved drink in Port Louis.

Bêti wished she was close to the grand bazaar to indulge in yet another refreshing brain freeze.

But for now, she had to face the melting pot of humans wading in all directions with a hasty step.

They packed themselves together, tight, under large umbrellas.

Everyone in the city seems to carry an umbrella, though more for shade than shelter.

Bêti made a mental note to follow her mother's advice and be indoors by noon.

People in the tropics retreat to cooler shaded areas and stay indoors when the sun is at its zenith.

Unlike the tourists on the island's beaches, they roasted themselves till they turned into a scarlet glow going indoors, only when the sun had gone down.

शहर – City

Plaine Verte's location breathed in a casual air and not parochial in attitude. Nestled at the eastern side of the city centre, this is where settlements started during the French colonial times.

It provided a passable education to whoever grew up on its narrow-paved streets, with a veneer of respectability and, most importantly, a convenient holding pen for middle-class children who, for one reason or another, required to be dumped somewhere, unobtrusive.

The landscape of Plaine Verte consists of small colonial houses, a few larger ones with inner gardens, and cool courtyards, tiny packed alleys with Lilliputian one- or two-bedroom dwellings right on the pavement. With more modern breeze block one or two storey buildings, mostly inhabited by the Chinese and the rest were commercial shops.

Bêti remembered her childhood spent there with a sweet ache in her heart. She found love there, one which gave her jelly knees, sweat along her back. It read a smooth coming of age with hues of emotions on a rollercoaster, never stopping to catch her breath. But the course of true love never did run smooth, and in her case, it meandered all over the place. The trouble was that she had more than her fair share of admirers: intellectuals and radicals mainly, even from the odd elite rich families. She was introduced to circles: long-faced, sincere men with shiny new ideas and baggy trousers wearing Dodo blue and raspberry flip flops who'd gather in tea houses around the main square and talk heatedly about the fraternal solidarity of the working classes and the dictatorship of the proletariat. Scores of sweet teas with gâteaux piments*, chana puris* and cassava puddings would come and go from the table without anyone noticing who had ordered them. Bêti never quite understood

* gateaux piments – chickpea chilli fritters
* chana puris – fried dumplings stuffed with mashed chana dal and spices

what attracted those male figures to her, as she considered herself to be very plain with her humble background. Like most radicals, the men talked a lot, but did nothing, and it didn't take an intellectual to see that she was tired of the endless discourse, despite her liberated views, what she really wanted was for a man to be a man. However, there was a line that was not to be crossed. She was a Hindu and the men were Muslim. Although fraternity and friendship were to the fore, dating was something which demanded more bravery.

That was something she didn't deem necessary to her present situation. It would bring too many complications and would just spoil things.

Besides, her interest sparked mainly on the intellectual ground, furthering it to the physicality of it, was only a quick put off for her.

She blamed it on the disintegration of the indentured workers, when many moved to the capital after the island achieved independence from British rule.

Families having toiled the land enough, sought different ways to earn a living.

The rich merchants from Surat offered jobs in their new trades they established along the main arteries of the city. These workers needed a place to live, and soon they started inhabiting this area off the grid, right after the city centre ended. It sprawled alongside river Tanier* and river Citron, making way for the less fortunate to rear some cattle and livestock.

The divide between Hindus, Muslims, Creoles and Chinese was the least felt in Plaine Verte. It held a spirit like none. Each person thrived upon the atmosphere of sharing beyond caste, creed and race. All festivals were celebrated fervently by one and all. Bêti had known this period in her childhood.

Men, she believed, are defined by the shadows they cast.

Most, despite the force of numbers and efforts, left little trace. Like ants toiling under the noonday sun, their shadows are picayune and ephemeral. Others, like the banyan trees with their dangling thick

---

* Tanier – Latanier river flowing from Le Pouce mountain across Port Louis in Mauritius

canopies, cast a shadow far greater, their penumbra eclipsing and influencing all who sat beneath. There are others still, a deadly few, who pass through invisible, yet leave everything altered in their wake. In a world marked by the shadows of men, it is those who have no shadow who are the most dangerous of all.

Bêti could not stop thinking how these huge banyan canopies alongside Magon gardens made her happy. Tall palms swayed to the gentle breeze; leafy Indian almond trees cast their shadows so cool they rivalled any air-conditioned room. One could dream with eyes open watching the vast blue cloudless sky with a glimpse of a lone paille-en-queue. Benches invited passers-by to sit down and take in the natural beauty plonked right in the city. Hibiscus bushes displayed endless colours of blooms, while flame trees woke up in splendour dressed in crimson, in the months of December to February. The clamour of the city, the traffic buzz didn't interfere with the serenity of the gardens.

All evolved around it.

Bêti gathered her thoughts and headed home. She passed through the narrow, cobbled stone street named after colonial figures. Port Louis was a gleaming, colonial town with white and grey buildings set around spacious squares and gardens. It oozed oriental charm with French architecture.

Bêti passed through the Chinese quarter. The streets were teeming with people and lined with shop-houses, their shutters painted in deep red shades. They were filled with every imaginable thing for sale, the goods jumbled in the windows and sometimes flowing out onto the pavements. Carts full of goods trundled past ornate Chinese temples, and exotic mosques with towering white and green minarets.

One day in Port Louis was enough to fill her head with questions and memories to last the week. She still was clueless as to where her maternal genes came from! She had to rely on the account of her great grandmother being admonished for being too fair … too white was the right word.

This was seen as a betrayal amongst the second generation of indentured immigrants. Almost like a curse had struck the family. Women behind their sari folds muttered that the progeny of such a woman would know no son, but a daughter befalling into sin. "And there I am" thought Bêti, born of the fourth generation, a daughter and still counting her sins. No son from my Mum's line. She wondered if any of these women in the past had uttered a curse which proved to be cast. And to stay!

It always seemed so strange to Bêti how, within the space of moments, life could go from being one thing to another thing entirely – with no hint, no warning sense of the change afoot. She had left her comfortable life to trace back the roots of her mother. A person she aches for every day of her life. Her mother and herself felt like two individuals with one life. With the passing of her a decade ago, finding out about her maternal links became almost an obscure obsession for her.

It was raining. An unusually heavy downpour for mid-afternoon. The sky turned the colour of iron through puffs of dense dark clouds, and the electric light had to be switched on, much to the dismay of Bêti.

Rain drummed loudly on the tin roof, and she had to turn up the volume of the tv. Some Bollywood song was playing, and the characters were thrown into contortions, shaking their limbs frantically, sometimes to the right, sometimes to the left, with the women swinging their hips. She followed the movements of the dancers yet looking through the emptiness.

A gentle breeze carried from the city, musty with pollen, dust and drains, the heat and sweat of hundreds of thousands of people. Her sleep was full of vivid dreams that night, and she woke early, happy they all ended when she opened her eyes to the new day. Her mind was still whirring when she woke, a pink dawn breaking through the shutters. She rolled over, listening to the birds chirping away in the garden, the repetitive swoosh of someone sweeping the veranda outside.

It was early, too early to be awake; she could tell from the muted light, the heaviness in her warm body. She stared through the white veil of her mosquito net, considered trying to get back to sleep, then, knowing she'd never be able to, pushed herself up, dressed, and crept quietly downstairs. Breakfast was already laid out in the shade of the veranda awning: freshly cut pineapple, guava and mango beneath a fly net, sliced baguette in a basket with butter in a glass dish, and bowls of creamy curd, honey and pistachio nuts, with the aroma of vanilla tea floating in the air. She heard her help in the kitchen, humming a song. The morning was announcing itself to be good. Maybe, it was time to reset her thoughts and spring to a next visit to the city, which she thought incapable of repeating after yesterday's tiring visit. But her quest could not be halted.

She made it to the spice market on her next trip. She had to draw a resolute breath before ducking through the low-beamed doorway into the cavernous rows of stalls. Why was she here? She had no idea, but somewhere she just responded to her instinct, and they led her to the heart of the city again.

She looked up from beneath the brim of her straw hat, eyes adjusting to the dim light, her ears to the intense noise: vendors shouting their prices, hundreds of locals haggling. The air was dense with trapped sunshine, a heady cocktail of chillies, saffron, turmeric and cardamom. A shirtless boy hared past, barrow full of coconut husks, and she stepped back clumsily, only just avoiding being mown down. Gathering herself, she walked on, down the first pungent alleyway of stalls, full of bags brimming with chillies, feeling the heat catch at her throat, her lungs.

One old man grinned at her and held out a dried chilli, gesturing for her to come forward.

'It good,' he said, 'no fire, this one.' She went, hesitantly, and took a small bite, fully expecting to lose the lining of her mouth.

'It is good,' she said, hearing her own relief.

'Yes,' she smiled, 'good.' Others called out to her, offering cinnamon, aniseed, all spice, poisson salé*, octopuses splayed, dried and hard. Incense, camphor, Hindu deities in brass, and lines of hanging multicoloured diaphanous paréos* ready for a customer to buy and take to the beach.

When Bêti woke this morning, she couldn't wait to get back to the cut and thrust of city commerce. The sugar, shipping and property interests, a solid base laid down in the eighteenth century on which future business could and would be constructed. This city probably hid what she was looking for, an answer lost in layers of generations led by colonial masters.

Sugar trade was not what it was. Bêti had known that for a long time. Thanks to Napoleon's encouragement, Europe was growing field after field of sugar beet. Transport costs were minimal compared to importing sugar from the colonies. The writing was on the wall. All she had to do was to read

---

* poisson salé – dried salted fish
* paréos – Beach wrap around

from the right clues. Where does she start from? The visit to the archives led to nothing.

She passed by a shop lit bright with ceiling lights and mirrors, a lady opened the door and a waft of cool air hit Bêti. She couldn't resist the temptation of cooling herself down for a moment and entered the shop, wiping off the sweat on her forehead.
A bevelled mirror sent back a reflection of herself. All she could see was a red flushed face. She looked around. Apart from the Chinese shopkeeper, everyone was of a burnished complexion. But none showed the effect of the heat in a pink blush.

Bêti thought that as usual, she had never seen anyone of colour, besides her, harbouring such a flush, surely this was a giveaway of something else racing in her pool of genes she had inherited from her Mum, who incidentally, also had pink cheeks from heat and her emotions.

A surly cat was lurking out there, not ready to give up the bones. Like the locals say *'anguille sous la roche'**

---

* anguille sous la roche – there's an eel hiding under the rocks

Chapter 2

मोहन – Mohan

Moonlight shone through the slatted shutters, throwing alternate bands of black and silver across the rich rugs and curtained bed.

Mohan was surfacing from a half-remembered dream, crossing over into that nebulous state where reality takes over and waking up is not so distant.

On the other side of the bed, his wife moved, ready to be giving birth, soon. Her distended belly seemed to burst at each movement she made.

Only in dreams could he see the child, the years to come when he would grow big and strong, learn to ride, to sail and to manoeuvre the hoe, just as his father had done. Although he tried to hold onto it, the dream would not stay, and he began to awaken. Through half-closed eyes he saw the familiar bars of light and dark. He liked this room, and the way the moon bathed it with light. He would normally have drifted back into sleep, but instead he jerked awake, aware that something had happened, though not quite sure what.

A rustling sound. Perhaps trees dancing before a sudden breeze, or sugarbirds disturbed from their night-time slumber. Alert now, he opened his eyes. The bars of light were suddenly interrupted by a fleeting shadow. He sat up.

Something or someone had rushed past the window. He leapt from his bed and threw open the glass shutters. The trees were still. Even the flock of birds sleeping on the branches of the huge mango tree didn't make a sound.

Suddenly, they dived towards the ground, fluttered and took flight again. Something had disturbed them. Someone was still out there.

Mohan reached for his clothes and headed outside. The whole house was sleeping, and although it occurred to him to wake someone, he decided not to. It would take too long and by then, whoever was lurking outside, would be gone. Trusting his fists for protection, he ran outside, the grass wet beneath his bare feet. Ahead of him a figure moved into the moonlight before disappearing into the trees. Avoiding the gravel path, he ran in that direction, legs made strong from years at sea, propelling him swiftly over the ground.

The figure had vanished.

The world seemed still; glades speckled with moonlight; he heard more rustling. He stopped and peered into the foliage, which wavered as though disturbed by a light breeze. Tonight, there was no breeze.

'Who's there?'

No sound came back. A cold shiver ran down through his spine. He felt a presence, but not a good one. Then, it all suddenly turned black. Next, Mohan was waking up in his bed. Had he walked back?

No.

A dream, a nightmare?

'Where did you find me?'

'In the bed, where else?' Said his very pregnant wife, Maude.

'I went out last night, to the bushes to the fields, then I blacked out and don't remember a thing.'

Maude moved on the rattan armchair by the bed, adjusting herself.

'Why do you think you left the bed?'

'Because I did!'

'Come on Mohan …. I would have known you know I have very light sleep these days. What are you trying to say?'

'Believe me dear, I saw something outside, and I went to look, a form swiftly ran to the fields, I followed it and …. You know, I am now waking up in bed. Did someone bring me inside?'

'Oh, now you are scaring me! If it all happened as you say, don't you think you would have woken me?' Frowned Maude.

'Recently, there have been some rumours of a Daïne* on the prowl again …. I believe your being with a child is no coincidence of that presence I saw and felt last night.'

---

* Daïne – a female ghoul

'Can I get you a cup of chai my love? Maybe you need to wake up properly from god knows what dream you are still in ….'

Mohan looked out to the morning light outside and gave a big sigh.

'A Daïne …. who would have thought that I would believe in such stories?' Deep inside he was shrinking in fright. All the past stories of daïnes he has heard from childhood came to his mind.

'What is a Daïne?' Maude asked nonchalantly, not realising with what gravity her husband just spoke. She was a French white who had eloped with a Hindu sirdar who worked on her father's sugar estate.

Mohan started coming to their house to fix certain things and also bring regular fish on Fridays as he was a part time fisherman. The young woman was smitten by this tall dark handsome Indian who also reciprocated to her feelings. It didn't take them long to understand that it was lethal for such a relationship to have any future. Severing it or eloping, Maude chose the latter.

Here she is ever since, living the love story of her life in a shack with the man she loved the most and now about to give birth to their child. She had not been long on the island to understand all the jargon of the locals, although she picked enough Patois Créole and Bhojpuri to get by on a daily basis.

'Daïne' what was that exactly? And why was Mohan so shaken up?

Mohan continued to remain silent during mealtimes from that incident. He could not stop worrying about Maude and his unborn child. Marrying her had been the best thing that had ever happened to him, but there it was. The island came with its own threats.

He had heard of Daïnes who were on the lookout for unborn babies to take and kill. The supernatural beliefs of the island are cushioned in African, Indian and European folklore.

It is believed that Daïne, also known as Churel, lives in an area of the village, and an evil spirit resides within them. Villagers believe these women destroy everything good. They are reported in and around cemeteries, abandoned battlefields, crossroads, toilets and squalid places.

A churel is a vengeful ghost that arises from the death of a woman during pregnancy or childbirth, with preternatural powers similar to a witch. Indian witch stories are common across the country.

Mohan decided to confirm his doubts and fears about having encountered a Daïne the other night. He couldn't tell Maude given her situation and the young woman wouldn't understand his fears.

A week later he cornered Baptiste, his fellow fisherman with whom he shared the boat and asked him whom he could have seen running away.

'There's only one way to be sure, let me take you to my grandmother, she's very well versed in these sorts of things.'

'I don't know who it was, Baptise.'

Mohan, who was surely in his mid-twenties, shook his head. His eyes were round with worry, and he looked in any direction rather than meet Baptiste's eyes.

'Trust me. Please!' Something in the tone of his voice had an effect. Baptiste squirmed and thought about it.

'I can't tell you for sure,' he said eventually.

'You know how it is.'

He nodded at Mohan and licked his lips. He was obviously nervous about saying anything.

There were some dangerous people on the island. Eloping with one's master's daughter was only for the crazy and the brave. Intimidation hadn't ceased with slavery, neither with indentured workers. Humanity puts up its own barriers to true freedom. Toe the line or you cease to belong.

'Am sure, someone was just checking on your wife … don't worry about it. However, if you think about what you suspect it is, then you should be cautious.'

'My grandmother will know, let's go and see her.'

Mohan looked at Baptiste with concern.

'The Master will know about his daughter being pregnant and her whereabouts, it's too dangerous. No, your grandmother can get ….'

'They won't hurt her. She's too old and knows too much about the old ways. They're frightened of her.

She lives in the old slave compound near Rivière du Poste'

Mohan knew the place; she had heard of it during many conversations among men gathered around at the end of the day for a fag and gossip.

Shacks that had once housed slaves were slowly being reclaimed by the wilderness. The trees were thick there, the last remnant of an ancient forest.

'I thought that place was long abandoned.'

Baptiste smiled and admiration shone in his eyes.

'Not by her.'

The old slave compound at Rivière du Poste was approached by a narrow path that wound through thick undergrowth of acacias. Little sunlight penetrated through the overhead canopy of tangled branches. Brightly coloured birds and butterflies flashed through the gloom and Baptiste chased them with his hands.

Matante* Clara's house was built of rough stone, with a roof thatched of palm and dried sugar cane leaves. A plume of smoke crawled skywards from a black cast iron marmite that looked as if it had been stuck on as an afterthought. They saw a few red hens throwing a loud cackle while scraping the ground with their claws in a resolute search for food.

Baptiste poked his nose forward and shouted, 'Matante Clara? Cote toi?'

The silence was strangely deafening. Mohan kept his gaze fixed on the lop-sided door of odd-sized planks, which were nailed together in a haphazard fashion.

'Perhaps she's dead,' whispered Mohan. Baptiste told him to be quiet.

''You are members of the La Tour family?' The voice was high-pitched, oddly attractive and took them unaware. Mohan looked at Baptiste, astounded.

'How did she know that?' Baptiste shrugged. Maude was indeed a De La Tour.

'Can we come in Matante?'

---

* matante – aunty in French creole

'You are already in, why are you asking me?

Be careful with my door.' There was no sign of wavering in her voice, no thin wail of old age. Baptiste opened the door carefully, catching a piece of wood as it slid off its frame. He leaned the whole thing against the side of the hut, bent his head and entered. Mohan followed. The hut was small, the floor was packed with mud and the shutters were made of woven grass. There was a bed made from saplings, its mattress a single blanket tied with string to the frame. A cooking pot hung from a tripod over a bed of glowing embers. A curtain of mauve muslin hung from the wall, though on closer inspection Mohan saw it was a dress of the style women wore at the turn of the century. The cloth had yellowed in places and it looked in danger of falling to pieces, but at one time it had been beautiful.

Matante Clara was tiny. She was sitting in an armchair that might once have graced a plantation mansion. The wooden arms were shiny from years of use, their lion heads polished by years of restless hands. The old woman's bare feet hung ten inches short of the floor. Her eyes were like glossy black buttons gazing out from sunken hollows, and her face was a mass of wrinkles, like the tough skin of an old pear. She waved her hand as though bidding them to sit down.

'Assizer!' *

Mohan looked for some non-existent chairs and he squared himself on the floor. The silence, the sound of insects and birds and the rustling of dark-green foliage in an itinerant breeze made the heat seem more than usually oppressing.

Unblinking, her gaze stayed fixed on his face.

'Are you here to stare at me in the face or tell me why you are here?'

'Matante,' started Baptiste, 'in fact, Mohan pretends he saw a Daïne the other night,'

'A Daïne!' Shirked the old hag.

'What makes you believe so? Is your wife pregnant or dead?' Mohan was thrown back by these statements and felt his throat parched.

---

* Assizer – take a seat

'How did you know?'

'Dead or pregnant? You tell me'

'She's pregnant …' heard Mohan say with a slight stammer.

'There was a woman of Africa, brought 'ere to be a slave. One day, she wanted fuel for her cooking pot and didn't have any. Nor did she have the money to buy any. Desperate she was, and 'her children were hungry, so she stole some charcoal and got found out.'

The old woman paused.

'This woman was fierce for her children. Fierce for their lives. When she got found out, she proclaimed she didn't care; that she'd die for her children if need be. It was the worst thing she could have said. She wasn't regretful about what she did, you see. She wasn't regretful at all, and the master, Missier Blanc, was angry. So, they cart-whipped her.'

A kind of adverse loyalty to plantation owners, and more particularly to the de La Tour family, made Mohan want to protest that this couldn't be true, that no man could do this to a mother who simply wanted to feed her family. But the words stuck in his throat.

'You know what that means?' she asked him. He nodded. 'That means they tied her to a cart to whip her. In front of everyone, her children, her husband …. they saw her bare back turn bloody with deep grooves left from the lashes.'

A heavy silence hung in the air.

Baptiste shrugged. 'I didn't like hearing all that about whipping. It makes me feel uncomfortable.'

Mohan nodded grimly. 'It should make us all feel uncomfortable. A civilized man shouldn't have such a thing in his history. It's a blot on the soul.'

He fell silent again. He clearly didn't want to be reminded that De La Tour's wealth was based on sugar and enslavement of others. He felt guilty to have married the master's daughter.

To infringe upon uncharted social areas during such epochs was either sheer betrayal or showing guts to uphold a human equalized way of life. On one side was a super comfortable rich lifestyle with all the lavishness it brought, on the other, was the workforce sharing the fate of cattle with no regard nor empathy to their conditions. Such was a colonial island at the hands of whites with coloured slaves at their beck and call. And Mohan has picked the most beautiful woman in that crowd of riches. And now, he was afraid for both his and her lives as well as that of their unborn baby.

Matante spoke:

'That wife of yours, is she ready to give birth? Send her to her parents; generally, the Hindus know what to do to avail themselves of Churels. But whatever you do, you should do it quickly.

Daïnes and Churels hit their victims 10 days before the birth. From now on, tell your wife not to leave the house after sunset. No potting around in the garden either.

Do not get her near a cemetery or crossroads! Give her a pair of scissors to keep under her pillow when she sleeps.

You see, Churels have long hair, which is where their strengths reside, and the sight of a knife or scissors scares them off enough not to approach you. Your wife should always wear her underwear inside out. It acts like a deterrent to try and get to the baby.

 Don't ask me how? I don't know.

Churels or Daïnes have a thirst for bleeding pregnant women, so if she ever bleeds, ask her to burn her underwear along with her sanitary cloth. That's all for now, I shall tell you more when I can figure out what kind of Churel we are dealing with here.'

'There are different kinds of Churels?' Asked Baptiste.

'Oh yes! Many types of these damned spirits. But, Mohan, you need to send her to her Malabar parents. They are good at dealing with Churels, their priests know what to do.'

Mohan suddenly felt his limbs go cold and a frisson gripping his nape.

'She is not Hindu, …. and I can't send her to her parents, as she eloped.' 'Ayo bon dié!* …there we go. She must be a Créole then, send her back, and tell her

---

* Ayo bon dié – Oh My God in French Creole

to get rituals done to protect her and the baby from Daïnes'.

Baptiste responded quickly, and advanced to Matante with imploring hands.

"Matante Clara, my dear friend, has real big problems.... only you can help him. You see, his wife is not Hindu .... nor Créole either ..." he started pleading, knowing that he would trigger the wrath of the old hag.

'So, what is she?! A regal Blanche? Don't tell me ...hahaha'

'Indeed, that's what she is,' Mohan whispered. With a swift movement, the old lady turned to him, with her twinkling eyes under her furrowed brow, wrinkling her leathery mahogany skin more.

'What are you talking about?! If you think you have come to play and trick an old lady like me, you better behave! I shall whack your backsides so hard you will not remember your names ...I tell you!'

Both men fell silent and looked at each other with grave faces. Failing to reply back to her threat made Matante Clara understand what was really happening.

This idiot of Mohan was with a 'Madame' … heaven forbid it's not from Mons De La Tour.

'Yes, Matante, my Maude is Missier De la Tour's daughter'

'Ayo mo bon dié …Saint Zézi Sainte Marie, be ki to fine faire mon garçon*!'

'What do I do Matante? How do I protect Maude and our baby?'

Matante Clara seemed shaken by what she heard, got up from the chair, and went outside. The men followed her. She looked around her, sniffed the air, and looked up at the sky. Then, turning her back to go to the hut again, she asked them to come and see her again in two days.

Mohan's brow was distinctly furrowed as they walked back through the lush green vegetation that divided the old compound from the biggest cane field nearby. Powder-puff clouds spilled from the interior

---

* Saint Zézi Sainte Marie, be ki to fine faire mon garçon? – Dear Jesus, Holy Mary, what have you done my boy?

into a sky so blue he wanted to dive into it. The sun was warm, and vivid birds skimmed the tops of the cane spears. If the Garden of Eden had ever existed, it would have looked like this, thought Mohan. But right now, he felt he was at the brink of falling into hell. He felt a bitter taste in his mouth, and he hastened his steps. He wanted to reach home and be with Maude.

He was convinced that a bad spirit was stalking Maude, but so far, he had no clue as to how to get rid of this malevolent spirit. Matante Clara looked so frail and scared, what could she do in two days for Maude?

Despite the warnings from Matante Clara that it was dangerous to be out after sundown, Mohan walked through the darkness towards a house where climbing plants had run riot over a wrought-iron veranda. He settled himself in a rickety chair and eyed the dark silhouettes of trees against an indigo sky.

It has been barely a year since Maude and himself called a Hindu priest in secret and took their sacred vows of marriage, circling the fire seven times. Each one for one vow. They have since been living far from any settlements in this little house that he found and improved. Both of them have been very cautious and didn't socialise lest someone spots Maude and informs her father.

Fortunately, the little corner where they were living was surrounded by a small forest, where wildlife thrived. Their small vegetable patch provided enough for their daily needs.

Once a week, Mohan went to the next village to get some other staple foods. Other things were provided by Baptiste which he brought to the boat when they went fishing. Maude had adjusted to their simple lifestyle and never showed herself to be lacking in any comfort.

So far, the providence was with them, but now this Daïne is threatening their peaceful life.

मंदिर –Temple

In a scenic corner of the island, beside lilac silky speared sugarcane fields and across from a bois-noir* and tambalacoque wood, near rain-bejewelled coffee plants lined with chalta* trees and betel vines, a small temple nestles, slowly going to ruin. It has seen some good days when men and women came to pray here; but now it is hiding countless secrets deep within its crumbling walls.

Woodlice have burrowed into its pillars and fire anthills adorn its steps and cling to its small veranda. Cobwebs stretch from one end of the temple bell to the other. Once gleaming yellow, now tarnished rust; once heralding devotees and massaged by a thousand pious palms, now caressed by silvery cobwebs of

---

* bois noir – black ebony
* chalta – elephant apple, native to India

spidery secretions and frantic with the frenzied patter of trapped insects. A huge banyan tree had conspired to form a canopy over the temple, hiding it from the world. Warm air, infused with the zesty tang of ripening fruits and the smokiness of nearby sugar factories, hangs respectfully around the mandir, loath to disturb the sombre peace.

A dilapidated cottage is just visible between the columns of deciduous roots gracing the temple courtyard, which are almost as tall as the overgrown trees to which they belong.

The disintegrating, moss-steeped walls of a cottage glow orange-gold in the shafts of sunlight occasionally piercing the vibrant green awning of branches, playing hide-and-seek with the insects that scurry around.

The wall of tumbledown basalt rocks surrounding the temple and the cottage is almost completely covered with velvet moss.

From certain angles, with its foliage-festooned steps leading up to its open cave of a mouth, lush vegetation parting to afford a tantalising glimpse of the deity within with wide eyes, its small shrine draped with vine and creeper garlands, its offerings of rotting leaves, the temple looks as if it is smiling; a slumbering child experiencing happy dreams.

माँ – Mother

Bêti came back home after another hot aimless search in the steamy capital. Reaching her room, she closes her eyes and leans against the wall as she catches her breath. She wants to strip down to her underwear and lie down under the fan. She wants to open the fridge and sit down inside like a cat to cool down.

She remembers her Maman and wants to hide in the folds of her sari skirts like she used to as a child breathing in the scent of talc, comfort and her 'maa'. It was unfortunate that so far, none of her searches were leading to any track. She still couldn't offer a posthumous face of her grandmother to her mother.

Maybe there was none.

Maybe she abandoned her child upon birth? who knows? ...

Maybe it was a truth too painful to endure that it had to be ended in the way it did. Leaving years and years of unanswered questions.

'What would you do if you found out the truth, Maa?' She thought aloud.

Outside, the world moves on, Bêti is catapulted back into childhood and young adulthood. No matter how far she goes, she can never outrun her mother's upsetting moods. The latter would sit by herself, thinking of her own mother of whom she could not even remember her face. It might hurt her departed soul more now, if the bland statement hiding a truth her mother should have never known came forth.

She sighs deeply, then pulls herself together.

'I might be defeated but I am not giving in. I have no choice but to go back, yes, until I figure out what it is about the non-existent records of my great grandmother.'

She looks outside and sees the gardener who is half-heartedly tending to the plants, the hibiscus shrubs full of pink, orange and white flowers bestowing blessings alongside the sunny smiles of orange marigolds.

She pictures the sprawling villas that were the plantation owners' residences during colonial rule, with spacious rooms looking out onto manicured lawns and sometimes, a coffee estate beyond. She loves to walk among tall coffee plants, the plump, lush beans turning from green to red, some yellow, the taste of burgeoning life with the bitter undertone of ripening coffee. It grew mostly in the highlands, where it was much cooler. The island has many of such villas. Could one of them be hiding a secret about her great great grandmother's ancestry? For as far as she remembers, nearly all the indentured immigrants who were brought to the island were recorded. If one does not figure on the workers records, it would mean the person wasn't a manual worker. What if it happens to be one of the ruling class?

'Yes! Why didn't I think of this? Now that makes more sense. I have been looking for records of Maman's ancestry in the wrong place.'

Bêti knew she had stumbled upon a stark possible reality. Hidden for multiple decades, even centuries. She could picture the local women of the time, seeing a white woman with an Indian man. The hot, sweet smell of perspiration and fresh gossip. Awed whispers growing, becoming rumbles, spreading outwards. Till where did it reach?

Shouting a story that nobody knows but everyone wants to claim, to narrate. Of something that doesn't happen every day. Her own great great grandmother must have been from the family of a white sugar estate owner. Bêti had a flash of her mother who was a single parent, but never complained about her husband who left her for another woman.

Her Maman kept people at bay. She had many acquaintances, but no friends. Single and very pretty, she never dated anyone. She rebuffed admirers. She was a quiet, self-contained, prickly person. She held her head high with a lot of resilience and dignity. One can say she was solitary. Not lonely. She was always on the go. She kept herself too occupied to be lonely.

But she was alone. Apart from her daughter, she had nobody.

Beti always got the feeling she preferred it that way, that she actively sought this distance from people.

Bêti didn't have a father or extended family. No grandparents, uncles, aunts, or cousins. Her mother made sure there was no one who would disturb her daughter's life by prodding the painful separation she had with her husband.

'I miss you Maman, I want answers from you.'

She feels like she's abandoned her just when she desperately needed her, although she knew, of course that dying wasn't her fault. For days, months and years, she remained in limbo, cocooned in grief and anger.

Emotions when one is comfortable with and actively seeking, so one doesn't have to move forward into the unknown, face the world, without your mother.

Now, more than ever, she wanted to give answers to her Mother, and felt bitterly hurt that she never did anything when she was alive.

Bêti decided to pen her departed Maa a letter, she went to her bag to get a pen and found a notepad in her drawer. She began writing in her neat cursive handwriting.

'You loved me so much, Maman. More than I can fathom. I kept badgering you about the past, until what you were keeping from me was all I could see. My father never lifted a finger for me, nor for you, but for you, the past didn't matter. Nothing mattered except me. I was your life. This was what you tried to tell me, but I didn't understand. I thought you were being difficult. All my life, I fixated on what wasn't there, what was missing, pushing you away in the process. I never once thought to see what was there, right in front of my eyes.
Your daughter'

Bêti takes the page from the notepad, folds it and puts it in her bag. She looks at the three items she always carries, each remarkable in their own way, tucked in her back pocket.

A wooden mirror, a pair of gold hoop earrings and an ID photo. She sees her mother in them, growing taller than her. Her face turns sullen as she navigates the bittersweet milestones of adolescence towards adulthood.

Until one day, she left her and went abroad.

Hearts broke, hurt unspoken and the unspeakable happened. Two halves of the same soul got separated.

Chapter 3

चूरेल – Churel

A metallic smell filled the cabin, that of blood, and the old witch screamed. After nearly nine months of a sickening pregnancy, active labour had begun. As contractions arrested her body, she found her mind wandering to the past century of her despicable life. She had lived in the village ever since she could remember, but the villagers had never accepted her. They had not appreciated what she had done for them, for the safety which she had provided. It came with a cost, sure it had, but they never understood this. It was through an act of trickery that she was even able to receive the seed responsible for this child; and the man who had implanted it, would pay dearly for what was about to come. For she knew now that the child would not survive, his seed clearly too weak.

She pushed irately, cursing the farmer. Blood-fused tears streamed down her face, zigzagging through the maze of wrinkles which embellished her skin. Her muscles felt taught, as if her body were being stabbed with red-hot knives. She had known that the birth would be painful, for she knew all, she was a witch, after all, but this was far beyond even what she could imagine.

Things had gone wrong. Still, she would not give up just yet. She would give birth to this child. The baby crowned, as her skin tore with the ease of an autumn leaf. She pushed and ejected most of the length of his diminutive wrinkled body. Numbness cloaked her every nerve, the pain suddenly dull and pointless as though it no longer mattered. A baby boy. He gasped for air, then let out a long cry.

Soon after, he fell silent, the tiny movements that she had felt, now still. Static. Her son had not survived.

The witch's breathing grew laboured, and she cried out forlornly. She felt dizzy out of all the loss of blood with the delivery, knowing somehow that her own death was just moments away.

It was not the act of birth that would kill her. It was the loss of her son, the only thing that she had wanted in life. The only thing she had ever loved, from the moment she had first felt his movements. Yet, she felt at peace with this, knowing that this would all soon be at an end. This brief period of respite lasted just seconds, as the numbness faded, and the pain returned with the intensity of a thousand burning suns.

Before she even realized this had happened, both feet jerked swiftly in opposite directions, as naturally as if she were just bending her elbow at its joint, but ending with her toes pointing backwards, her heels forward. Bones and tendons broke, cracking with a frightening ease. Her eyes rolled back into her head, and she let out a bellow so loud that it shook the forest which surrounded her hut, in the sugar cane camp. Terrified of what she might see, she looked hesitantly down at her feet.

She vowed that she would ensure that no woman about to give birth like her would not go through this agony. She would make sure that she alleviated them of their suffering before it was too late.

Any man giving such woes to a woman from his seed would see no sunrise ever in his life.

After a cursory glance of the horror that had just ensued, she watched as her vision disintegrated into nothingness. By the time the villagers had discovered her body days later, it had turned black.

A Churel was born.

Bêti had a bad night. She tossed and turned in the empty bed, too large for her. Day will soon bleach the horizon. She will face the coming dawn despite the fear she has carried for more than fifty summers. Dawn has always brought loss. And yet this sunrise felt restorative. The charred sky catches its new flame. She reaches for its warmth, its peace, whatever forgiveness it might offer. As the first surge of daylight spills across the sky, Bêti stands beneath it with the eyes of a child, drinking it in.

Her island is suddenly with her the same gash of pink sky, the smell of cut cane at daybreak, the hands, the faces, the voices that have lived inside her for decades.

Memory lives in light, she thinks. Benevolence and redemption, too. But light illuminates all, even the darkened hollows. The sundials' mad circles have slowed, and the time for concealment has run out. Secrets are wild birds. They cannot be held captive forever.

> *Although I conquer all the earth,*
> *Yet for me there is only one city.*
> *In that city there is for me only one house;*
> *And in that house, one room only;*
> *And in that room a bed.*
> *And one woman sleeps there,*
> *The shining joy and jewel of all my kingdom.*
> *Mother.*

A soft vintage Bollywood song crackled on the radio, while Bêti made herself some vanilla tea with two teaspoons of powdered milk. The islanders drink their tea very milky and also very sweet.

Sugar - they had an abundance of it, in all its forms. Virtually colouring all that's green on the island. Vast patchworks of all shades of green stretch till the eyes can meet the horizon. It was Green then blue of the sea.

Terracine was a hamlet so small, so insignificant, it would be much too generous to describe it as a dot on the map. It sat near the coastal town of Souillac which was bathed in the most dramatic waves crashing at the highest cliffs of the island. Terracine happens to house one of the earliest settlements of the sugar estate houses for indentured workers called 'camp'.

Children of the hamlet ran barefoot in the muddy paths alongside the sugarcane fields, shouting, playing with abandon while their parents thanked the gods for this relief to have a roof over their heads and a meagre meal each day.

The wide blue sky flooded the nearby irrigation canals, hiding 'brèdes Martin*' and 'malbar*' while other plants jostled for the sun. Summer in the tropics

---

* brèdes Martin – edible greens of the nightshade family with a bitter taste, very popular in Mauritius.
* malbar – Indian Night shade, edible variety

is long and hot. It was not long before the fruit trees began to strain under the burden of their fruits.

Children climbed them all, the branches creaking from their weight, plucking and slurping ripened mangoes till the juice ran off and stained their chins. Sometimes they annoy macaque monkeys, by stealing their share.

Bêti had a distant Aunty who lived in Souillac, and she decided to pay her a visit. It will be a long drive down the furthest southern part of the island, but it might well be worth it. She knew that this Aunt's mum, when alive, had known Beti's grandmother.

Perhaps a little information might be pivotal in tracing that elusive track to find the answers she was searching for, concerning her mother. Only time will tell if the track would be fruitful in her search.

It all began with a bolt of lightning. Cutting through the stormy night sky, it crashed down on the roof of the most remote house, lost in the middle of sugarcane fields, no longer in use.

The young couple living there already knew it was to be a night like no other. What they didn't know was that a lightning bolt would set off a chain of tragic or perhaps miraculous events that no one ever could have imagined. Mohan, who had sought the knowledge and guidance from Matante Clara, was well aware of the impediment they were to face. But all this was still hours away. Whether she could have done something to change the course of events, or if everything was already predetermined with the arrival of the first drops of rain, was not something they could question at the time. With the second explosion of thunder, Maude felt a jolt in her lower body.

The baby moved constantly. In fact, the first contractions of labour had rolled in.

'Mohan...I think it has started. The baby is on its way'

Mohan threw a look of panic to Maude, he thought it had not been two days yet. Matante Clara was supposed to tell him what to do about Daïne. What now?

'Mohan, I need help from the village. I can't do this on my own, please find the local midwife.'

The throes of labour pain started to ride, making the young woman moan. She went to the kitchen with her arched back, grabbed a dekchi, filled it with water, and put it on the stove. Next, she dragged her feet to the chest at the feet of the bed and opened it. She pulled out some bedsheets and kept them on the nearby chair.

Mohan took his bicycle and rode to the village at full speed, getting splashed in the muddy potholes. By the time he arrived with Dadi Gopee, Maude was ready to be in full labour. The midwife examined her and got ready to set the delivery scene in the bedroom.

'Beta tu rahbé na?'*

Mohan replied with a confused look.

'Kaa Jeni Dadi, rehbé chahin ka?'*

---

* Beta tu rahbé na? – Son, you will stay back, right?
* Kaa Jeni Dadi, rehbé chahin ka? – I don't know Dadi, should I stay?

'Han, ego aur Jana habé ta thik baaté na'*

Baptiste could not be alerted to the unexpected delivery. What if the malevolent spirit was there? Mohan felt his hands and knees shaking. He was facing an unprecedented event and had no clue how to handle it.

The far reaches of the room stayed black with shadow. Maude was sweating profusely under the strain of labour, while she held Mohan's hand tightly turning his knuckles white.

Suddenly, a loud thumping at the door stunned everyone in the room. A dead silence filled the space, and Maude's moan stopped. She released Mohan's hand and whispered, 'Go, open the door;' the young man reluctantly got to his feet and slowly walked towards the door. When he opened it, Baptiste was panting, eyes wide opened.

'Baptiste! What are you doing here?'

---

* Han, eko aur Jana hobé ta thik baaté na – Yes, if there's someone else, it would be better, right.

'I heard about Dadi Gopee being solicited in the middle of the night and I knew it could only be you. Nobody in the basti is pregnant at the moment, requiring a midwife. So, I ran to Matante Clara, she sent me to fetch Marday, the priest. He moved to the side and a small skinny Tamil man showed himself in the dim light.'

'Come in, come in..' ushered Mohan hastily. Marday joined his palms and greeted Dadi and Maude.

'Vanakkam*, I am Marday, the iyer*'

'Namasté' replied Dadi with a frown.

'What are you doing here? This is no place nor time for a man to be here, except Madame's husband.' 'I was summoned for the Churel…' started Marday.

Dadi Gopee stopped short and looked at the priest with eyes like saucers.

'Churel! Are you out of your mind?! Do you see any churel here? This is a woman in labour about to deliver a baby'

---

* Vanakkam – greetings in Tamil
* iyer – priest in Tamil

'That's precisely why I was summoned. I was told by Matante to ward off a wandering Churel who might have been stalking Madame.'

Mohan couldn't have felt better. Ganesh bhagwan* has heard his prayers. Finally, some help has come forward. Thank you Matante Clara! he thought to himself.

'Well, Iyer, do what you have to do, but don't get in the way at all, it's a matter of life and death...in fact lives, I am responsible for both right now!'

'Dadi, I am also here to save their lives' replied Marday. To this, he pulled out a small packet from his pocket, went to the table and opened it. Mohan was watching him carefully.

'I will need some water in a lota*, some milk, and a knife.' Mohan promptly gave him all the things requested.

Maude opened her eyes and asked what was going on, Dadi comforted her and asked her to close her eyes

---

* Ganesh bhagwan – Lord Ganesha
* lota – pitcher vessel in hindi

and concentrate on her breathing. She rounded her shoulders up and down and back and forth then rolled her head from side to side until her neck cracked.

Marday went outside with the water vessel, and white mustard seeds he brought with him. Mohan followed him and stayed discreetly out of the way.

Marday started an incantation while burning a camphor square on the two sides of the doorstep, then went around the hut and did the same on each corner of the cardinal directions.

He then made an exploding sound 'Phat!'

Throwing the mustard seeds, he scattered them in the four directions. He comes into the house and repeats the same. Maude had started screaming and Dadi was busy helping her with the delivery.

'You both need to go out now!'

Mohan looks at Marday forlornly, the latter gently nods and they both exit the room. Outside, the cicadas were cacophonic and the inky sky above was a huge blanket of blinking stars. The air was balmy, and the night jasmine scent was numbing. Marday pats Mohan's back and says everything will be alright.

After a long silence, Mohan hesitantly asks Marday, 'what did you just do? Will Maude and the baby be safe now?'

'I have done my bit, the rest is up to the almighty, but don't worry, I have seen worse and I can tell you this always works.'

'What is this, Iyer?'

'You see, to ward off a churel, you need to find the spot where she died. The spot is then sown with mustard sarson*, which is also sprinkled along the road traversed by the corpse on its way to the burial ground. The reason behind this, is that the mustard blossoms in the world of the dead, and the sweet smell pleases the spirit and keeps her content, so that she does not long to revisit her earthly home.

Secondly, the Churel rises from her grave at nightfall and seeks to return to her friends but when she sees the minute grains of the mustard scattered, she stoops to pick them up grain by grain, and while she is engaged, the sun rises and she is unable to visit her

---

* sarson – mustard seeds

home. However, in this case, we ignore where she came from, hence I have barricaded any entry to the baby and the mother by sealing both interior and exterior. It is imperative to do this before the baby is born, because, heaven forbid, if anything happens to the mother, she can turn into a churel too, while the baby can still be born.'

Mohan shuddered and felt cold and shivery despite the balmy night. So, that was it, such a simple ritual and yet potent to ward off a malevolent spirit like a churel.

'So, ...this churel will not come now?'

'Oh no, she is always on the prowl, but she can't come here anymore. By this time, the baby will be thankfully born and out of danger.'

'I cannot thank you enough, dear Iyer, and forever grateful for what you have done for us. For my baby ...my wife ... sobbed Mohan.

A baby's cry was heard. Mohan jumped up.

'Go and see your newborn, I will get going now,' said Marday, as he rose and turned his back to disappear into the dawn.

Churel didn't claim any victim, Mohan couldn't believe his luck and rushed to his wife and newborn. Life never felt so precious.

Chapter 4 - Port Louis

"From the experience of all ages and nations, I believe, that the work done by free men comes cheaper in the end than the work performed by slaves. Whatever work he does, beyond what is sufficient to purchase his own maintenance, can be squeezed out of him by violence only, and not by any interest of his own." – Adam Smith

A shop in La Reine street caught Beti's eyes. It looked professional from the outside as Bêti walked past. It was a mixture of old and new.

The building was obviously ancient, but it had four large bay windows all crammed with brightly coloured surf, textile, and skateboards. There were mannequins kitted out in the latest sports gear and accessories. There was a huge black canvas sign over the top of the windows with the company logo and name.

Above each window hung a separate canvas with smaller signs reading 'hardware', 'clothing', 'accessories', 'free internet'. As she walked past, she noticed there were boards and branded posters hanging from the ceiling inside.

An old Miyaji* sat on a beautiful wicker chair.

Bêti felt attracted to it the moment she saw it. It was love at first sight. The chair had an elegant sloping back, a bit like a modern reclining chair, and a long seat - so that when you sat in it, your body slid down into a half-sleeping position.

The wicker was woven in diamond shapes and had a tinge of yellow, like hay; the armrests, made of teak, cradled your arms from the elbow to the fingertips.

Best of all were two discreet hinges below the armrests where two planks, rather like flat boat oars, were attached; they could be released and pulled forward to extend the arms. It was an unusual feature which puzzled her of its real use.

---

* miyaji – elderly Muslim cleric

It was this part of the chair that was most interesting to Bêti, because when you swung out the oars you could also make them meet in the middle, forming a bridge where the sitter could rest their legs and watch the world go by. She remembered having spent long Summers sitting in the veranda in her home in Port Louis on one such armchair.

'Bonjour Chacha, ki manière?'* Greeted Bêti.

The old man with a white crocheted prayer cap, lifted his eyes and looked hard at Bêti. He must be struggling to recognise this young woman through his decades of unfailing presence by this spot watching throngs of humans pass by. How could he remember her?

'Bonjour, mo bien …. ki sane la ou? Mo pas pe reconet ou?'

'Mo mama ti pe vine acheter bane zaffaire ici, Devika, ou rappelle li?'*

---

* Bonjour Chacha, ki manière? – good morning Uncle, how are you doing?

The old man scratched his head under his cap, out came a few strands of silvery white hair. His eyes suddenly activated and shone with interest.

'Ah sa ti Madame la sa, non? Avec sari?'

'Oui, li même, mo so tifi.'

'Hein ….! Ayo Bêti mo pas fine reconet toi, excuse moi, fine vine vié astere, lizier pas trop bon'*

Bêti crouched in front of the old man, and touched his hand, reassuring him, it was alright. She explained to him that she was on the island in the quest of demystifying her mother's ancestry. Chacha Moussa, as he was called, explained that many indentured people either lost their roots due to badly written, misspelled entries or the records themselves not surviving the countless cyclones and bad weather. The government was to be blamed for never ensuring that these precious records were housed in prime condition and cautiously handled.

Bêti bid goodbye to Chacha Moussa before heading to the archives. Arriving there, the doorman recognised her instantly and allowed her in without any hesitation. This time he did not tail after her. The archivist looked bright and refreshed in her pastel almond green saree and blouse with matching artificial pearls. She reminded Bêti of a cool Alouda. in fact, thinking of it, the young woman thought, this time, she will make a detour by the bazaar to "Pillay Alouda" to quench her thirst.

Bêti knew what she wanted to consult, and the archivist took her to the aisles and gave her the references. Fortunately, the huge ceiling fan was breezing them cool enough to stand the hours of research in this heat.

Bêti started reading from an old musty smelling, Ivory vellum stack of papers drafted in old French cursive handwriting. There were countless pages of the French Colon families settled in various parts of the island.

Her reading continued till it was time for the shutters to come down. She made notes while reading and she would go through them again, once home. She managed to catch a glass of Alouda on her way back before tumblers and pails were stocked for washing.

Everyone was ready to pack and go home. Summer days can feel long in the capital.

"In 1715, Mauritius was claimed by France, but it wasn't until 1721 that French settlers from Reunion made a first attempt at settling the island, which they named Île de France. During the first years of French rule, a multi-ethnic population was created as people from India, Madagascar, Europe, African countries, and China were moved to the island.

An attempt was made to develop agriculture, but just as had been the case during Dutch rule, cyclones, droughts, and pests made this quite an unsuccessful endeavour. Slaves as well as some workers and soldiers escaped into the forests from which they would frequently launch attacks.

Soldiers often refused to take orders, and many of those who did stay faithful to their governor, were heavy drinkers. Just as had been the case with the

Dutch, in the first decade of French rule, the settlement was on the verge of collapsing.

The tide quickly turned when Bertrand-François Mahé de La Bourdonnais took up his post as governor of Île de France and Île de Bourbon (Réunion) in 1735.

He brought discipline back to the population and created several businesses for which he often provided the starting capital. Sugar, indigo, cotton, and tobacco plantations were set up, and an adequate labour force imported from India.

Port Louis was transformed into a well defended naval base with a state-of-the-art naval workshop, where stores, a market, a theatre, an aqueduct, and a large hospital were built.

During the latter part of the 1730's, a large number of infrastructures were constructed as well.

Slaves were offered training in activities such as shipbuilding and stone cutting.

Moreover, they were enrolled as slave hunters and were given a salary. They became very effective in reducing the runaway slave population. La Bourdonnais was replaced in 1746.

The following two decades agriculture developed further. Just when Île de France seemed to develop a self-sufficient food production; the Seven Years War broke out in 1756. Large numbers of French soldiers on their way to India called at Mauritius, and quickly the island was threatened with starvation.

The war ended in 1763, and four years later the French government bought Île de France from the East India Company. By this time, 18,777 people, of which over 15,000 were slaves, populated the island. By the end of the eighteenth century, this amount had more than tripled, with slaves constituting over 80% of the island's population. It is estimated that a total of 160,000 slaves reached Mauritius and Réunion between 1670 and 1810, of which 87% came from various regions in Africa and 13% from India.

In 1787, Port Louis was made into a free port, open to ships of all nations. This caused the number of merchants based in Port Louis to rise from 103 in 1776 to 365 in 1803.

During the late eighteenth century, ships from Asia, Africa, Europe, and the Americas brought in various commodities. These included foodstuffs such as rice and wine, textiles, goods required for the maintenance of ships, furniture, ceramics, luxury goods, and most importantly, slaves.

It was during this time that the harbour and dockyard were further developed, its equipment modernized, and cleared of silt and shipwrecks. Timber houses in Port Louis were replaced by ones made of stone and streets were paved.

Barracks and hospitals were constructed for about 2,500 troops, and Port Louis was steadily growing in size.

By the early nineteenth century, Ile de France was exporting a large variety of products, including coffee, indigo, tea, textiles, cloves, cinnamon, nutmeg, and ebony. Imports included wine and other liquor, salted food, ceramics, glass, and furniture.

During the American War of Independence, Île de France was again used as a major naval and military base for French campaigns against the British in India. Many soldiers and sailors, on their way to India, called at Port Louis, and this gave an enormous boost to the island's economy. Moreover, corsairs (as well as the French navy) based on Île de France plundered English merchant ships all over the Indian Ocean, which injected considerable sums of money into the island's economy. Merchants on the island engaged in trade with people from Europe, the Far East, the Middle East, and even the newly formed United States of America.

Due to its strategic position, Great Britain had its eyes set on Île de France. During the first decade of the nineteenth century, British ships occasionally raided the island and set up blockades to cripple trade with the outside world. In November 1810, the British arrived on the island's northern shores with a fleet of 70 ships carrying 10,000 troops. Over the years British spies had already gathered a lot of intelligence, and by the time of the invasion, the British were in possession of detailed maps of the island. The French, having only 2,000 troops, were greatly outnumbered, and capitulated on 3 December 1810.

The change of power was remarkably smooth, and people went on with their day to day business the day after the changeover. The island's upper class thought their financial interests would be best served by cooperating with the British, and immediately started to do so. One of the reasons for this was that the British had offered generous terms of capitulation: the island's laws, customs, religion, private property, free trade, and even the French language were respected. Under British rule, however, the island was once more named Mauritius. Agriculture was modernised by replacing human labour with machines and animals, the road network was improved, and the duty on sugar was reduced. As a result, sugar cane cultivation almost tripled between 1817 and 1827.

In the meantime, Britain saw a growing resistance to slavery, and the Mauritian planters feared they soon had to emancipate their slaves. The price of slaves had skyrocketed as ships of the Royal Navy tried to curtail the slave trade, which had been abolished in Great Britain's empire in 1807 but was still practiced illegally. In the meantime, though, the sugar industry was booming, and planters were in desperate need of cheap labour. To face the situation, they started to import indentured Indian and Chinese workers, who worked side by side with the slaves. In 1829, measures were taken to improve slaves' lives and racial segregation was abolished. Finally, on 12 June 1833, the British Parliament passed the Act that abolished slavery. After much resistance from the slave owners, a Proclamation was signed in January 1835 that introduced the apprentice system on Mauritius. Slaves kept on working as apprentices for a period of four years, after which they were emancipated, and the slave owners received compensation. Large numbers of ex-slaves were completely neglected by the authorities and fell victim to extreme poverty. In early 1839, just before all slaves were emancipated, the population of the island consisted of 9,000 whites, about 15,000 free 'coloureds', and 70,000 slaves. At this time, about 20,000 people were living in Port Louis.

Plantation owners continued to import Indian labourers to replace their freed slaves. Some parts of India were troubled so badly by unemployment, floods, epidemics, famines, and the oppression of certain castes that many people were keen to emigrate. The area under sugar cane in Mauritius rose from 42,000 acres in 1831 to 129,000 in 1861. The imports of Indians grew steadily, sometimes reaching over 40,000 people per year. By 1861, there were 193,000 Indians on the island compared to 117,000 whites and coloureds. The influx of Indian indentured labour ceased in 1909, with one last shipment of 1,500 in 1923 during the sugar boom of the early

1920's. The trade in Indian workers was, in many respects, not so different from the slave trade: workers were often recruited with brutal force; on their way to Mauritius, many died of disease. While on the island they were subjected to travel restrictions; and once they made it to the estates, workers were treated badly, including harsh corporal punishment and even imprisonment on estates. Like the slaves had done before, the Indians resisted the cruel system of which they were part. They frequently revolted, deserted, and went back to India.

During the first five decades of British colonial administration, the number of ships calling at Port Louis increased sharply due to a sugar boom and the construction of several ship repair facilities. In addition, the two railway lines were completed in 1864 and 1865. During the 1860's, the sugar industry in the Mascarenes began to decline. The number of sugar factories fell from 258 in 1860 to 66 in 1908. Plantations were frequently divided into small plots and sold; by the early twentieth century Indians had acquired almost one third of the land under cultivation. The 1890's proved to be disastrous: three epidemics, two fires, and one devastating cyclone laid waste to the island and its inhabitants. Moreover, the population had increased to 371,000 in 1901."

The capital wakes up slowly. By morning the dirt road usually clamoured with life outside municipal buildings; men and women lawyers in their black robes crossing the narrow pedestrian path to enter the palm ridden garden in front of the Supreme Court. A few streets away, farmers carrying produce to the grand bazaar auctions, scholars garbed in tie and carrying a briefcase with an air of seriousness in a hasty step, and Muslim elders with prayer beads strung around their wrists. There would always be a mob of children, faces burnt and glistening in the sticky heat, chasing one another down the street.

But not today.

Bêti is back again first thing in the early morning.

She stood by the seafront, watching as the fishing ships huddled next to each other steadily through the blue waters with light reflecting towards her. She slipped her jacket from her shoulders, releasing herself from the confines of its neat tailoring and letting the warmth of the Mauritian sunshine caress her skin.

Her arms were pale after the long northern winters she had endured in England; she felt like a butterfly, emerging from its snug chrysalis, suddenly discovering its wings and spreading them wide to soak in heat and light and colour.

A breeze, the soft breath of the wide Indian Ocean that extended to the other side of the world beyond the low-lying island, lifted her honey-coloured hair where it fell over her shoulders, cooling her neck and her flushed cheeks.

This morning felt like no other.

She had read quite a bit in the last few days to get a picture of what could have happened. Her great grandmother's name being non-existent could not have been an accident. It was intentional.

Chapter 5
Maude

Maude has been sitting under the veranda nursing her baby girl. It was a life changing experience for her, and she was finding her way to be a mother with no guidance from her own mother, so was not easy. She missed her presence so much and wished she could be closer to her. But her life with Mohan and her daughter would not allow this liberty. All through her life she felt close to nature, and the prospect of going to Mauritius after her schooling in Concarneau was most exciting. She dreamt of the exotic paradise after reading her mother's letters she sent regularly for all the years she was away from her.

Maude had travelled to the island on the ship route once before and could loosely recall the experience of being tossed about on a swirling sea, even though she had only been six years old at the time. She recalled tipping back her head to gaze up at the strangest of trees; all tall and skinny and waving their green fronds into the highest and bluest of skies. She remembered her eyes being dazzled and her face being scorched by the blazing sunshine. She remembered spinning around in a warm breeze, scented with flowers and sea salt and running on the beaches with her toes sinking in the powdery white sand. It had felt warm and not hard and cold as in Brittany. She was in love with the island where her parents owned vast amounts of land under sugarcane. Mohan was the most beautiful boy she had ever seen. He had golden skin and pale green almond shaped eyes and lustrous hair which shone like polished black granite, and it grew out from his head in thick coils. Mohan taught her to climb rocks and trees and to swim in the sea and to fish with a hand reel.

Over the summer she spent with her parents, they had become inseparable friends. One day, he'd given her a necklace that he'd made himself out of fine fishing twine, into which he'd set two very tiny but perfectly round white shells. He said he'd swam down and found them at the bottom of the seabed among the corals on the brizan*. He'd slipped the necklace around her neck and asked her to be his friend for life. She gave him her word. They sealed it with a peck on each other's cheeks à la Française.

A year or so later, however, her interest in him had shifted considerably when she went back to Brittany after the short holidays on the island. However, there were days when at school, she daydreamed about him and after class, when she was supposed to be doing her homework, she would stare out to sea from the window and wonder what he was doing right at that moment.

When she did see him again after many years, she couldn't help but notice how he was looking so much taller and that his previously skinny body and long thin arms had filled out with hard-toned muscle. He had facial hair too – a neatly shaped moustache above his top lip.

---

* brizan - reefs

Marie Noëlle, their housekeeper, had once said that Mohan had been abandoned on the beach as a baby by sea-gypsies, the nomadic people of the sea. And had been taken in by Bizlall, the coolie and his wife, who had raised him as his own. Sea-gypsies are generally feared by islanders, as they are thought to be thieves, raiders, and pirates. Some even think sea-gypsies have mystical powers and are able to conjure up curses and even hurricanes.

Of course, no one really knew the circumstances under which Mohan's mother had chosen to give him up, but Maude could only imagine that she must have been quite desperate to abandon her baby on a beach, in the hope he would be adopted by someone who might give him a better life than she could.

Maude believed in this story and she sympathised with Mohan's past, and it had cemented their special friendship. At that time on the island there had been lots of children growing up there, and Maude knew she wasn't the only girl to have noticed how Mohan had grown from a beautiful boy into a handsome young man. He kept on being around the estate villa as a handyman.

Other girls who visited her parents for parties and get-togethers, had curvier bodies than hers. They would openly flirt with him while they kicked a ball around with him at the beach. When she'd overheard one of these girls, saying to another, what she'd like to do with Mohan, given half a chance, Maude had felt sick with jealousy. Mohan belonged to her. Didn't he? Finally, unable to bear the agony of her secret crush on him any longer, while reel-fishing off the end of some dark basaltic rocks jutting out into the bay, she finally plucked up the courage to tell him how she felt. He'd stopped baiting his hook to look at her while she'd stood in front of him and stammered something about being ready to be his girlfriend and how she would quite like to kiss him, that is of course, if he would still like to kiss her? In one swift move he'd swept her into his arms, and he was kissing her for what seemed to Maude like forever. His lips were warm and soft and tasted slightly salty, and she could feel the heat of his body and the beat of his heart right next to hers. When they eventually stopped kissing, Mohan continued to hold her in his arms as the sun went down in all its splendour. They sat together closely entwined and watched the world around them change from blue to pink to red and then to gold and he stroked her hair with his fingers and told her she was the only girl for him in the whole world.

She had never been so happy.

It was a small island, however, and soon someone reported seeing the two hanging out together, far too closely. They soon were in trouble because of the strict division of class that existed between the former slaves, the indentured workers and the ruling estate owners. It was taboo to even think the two classes could mix; it was also about different ethnicities, which were like heaven and earth.

So, having been warned off seeing each other, they soon began meeting in secret. Maude would watch out for a small seashell left outside her bedroom windowsill, a signal that he was waiting for her at the hidden patch of sand between the huge basalt boulders at the end of the beach. Then checking carefully that the coast was clear, she'd sneak out of the window and across the open veranda to the side garden over the stone wall and drop down into the tropical fauna that would help to disguise her escape. This led to the grassy headland and down to a sandy path to the village and the small harbour with its plethora of shacks with ornate lambrequins and boat sheds built for the fishermen.

After two years of seeing each other in this stealthy way, tension started mounting in the villa.

One day, Marie Noële asked Mohan to stop coming, and that they had found a replacement in Ton Manev. The young man understood that things had gone too far, and this was a disguised warning from Marie Noële.

If the De Latour family took matters in their hands, it would mean total banishment and hardship for Mohan and his parents.

Maude reacted unexpectedly to this turn of events. One day, she went to meet him at the beach while he was mending the fishing nets with Baptiste.

When she returned to her house, a warm fragrance blew across her face and she turned towards the garden and tilted her face up to the sun.

Closing her eyes against the sharp yellow light, she inhaled the musky sweetness of the tropical garden around her where palm trees swayed with ripening coconuts under their fronds and bananas and starfruits hung heavy and ripe on the trees.

She tiptoed and entered the house tentatively and immediately appreciated a welcome coolness in the air and on her skin. In the reception hall there was a dresser upon which sat a bowl full of floating frangipani flowers.

Maude walked to her parents' room; it was far more spacious as it took up almost the entire length of the back of the house.

There were two sets of French windows along one wall that opens out onto the wooden deck of the first-floor porch. The room faced west towards the afternoon sun and inside it was oppressively hot and stuffy.

Maude immediately threw open both windows to let in a cooling sea breeze. She pulled back the long light calico drapes that were now billowing out like ship's sails and shading the room from the heat and brightness flooding into it.

She drank in the boudoir scene around her.

The oversized bed was covered with starched Indian bed sheets and with a mosquito net hanging above it. Two bedside tables each displayed faded photographs in mother of pearl frames and ornate lamps shaped like rearing seahorses with pale green silk shades. A row of sliding louvred doors along the opposite wall were broken up by the presence of a huge bookcase housing some of her father's favourite classic novels, her mother's collections of poetry, as well as an enormous leather-bound Holy Bible; her mother had been almost manically religious.

A last look at the bedroom, and Maude headed to her own. She lay spread out on the bed under the whirling ceiling fan and the quivering mosquito net and felt her body pulsating to the same rhythm of the tree frogs croaking in unison outside.

Perspiration trickled down her spine. Outside, she could see the light of day was already fading and the golden glow of dusk was starting to creep across the porch.

She had already closed the doors and was now sorely tempted to throw them open again to bring in a breeze but knowing that if she did so at this time of the evening, she'd also be inviting in swarms of hungry mosquitoes.

Her life was about to be changed for good. She was bidding goodbye to her house, and her current well sheltered life. A new one was waiting for her outside, in the humid heat.

She saw the face of Mohan smiling at her, holding her hand, and she felt happy again.

Yes, she had taken the right decision of leaving her parents' house for good and embracing Mohan.

The baby showed a face of irritation, Maude understood and went in to change her nappy. It was suddenly quite dark outside, and she remembered how the sun sank quickly over the horizon in this part of the world.

Mohan would be home quite soon, hopefully with a proper netting out for a good catch tomorrow early morning. She might have yet to eat some fresh unsold fish. She didn't complain, such bounty of fresh sweet gifts of nature was reason to be grateful.

Her life so far had been devoid of luxury and maids to attend to her, but the freedom and joy she experienced at each moment made all these appear quite trivial.

Life with Mohan and her baby was nothing short of being perfect.

Yet, a wrinkle of worry had turned into a frown every time she thought of what Mohan had asked her to do.

'Maude, Ma Cherie, I think that we should be careful what happens next to our child.'

'What do you mean?'

'It's, that ...hmm we should not disclose you as being the mother when we go for the registration at the civil status. This would endanger your life, her life ...' started Mohan softly.

'You mean, I should not write that I am her Mother?! ... I don't care what the world thinks of us.'

'You don't, but there are many who do, it's a cruel world outside.'

Maude was shaken by this request from Mohan.

Later, after having rethought it, she understood and accepted that he was right. It would be silly to threaten their quiet life with unreasonable trauma.

What Maude would do would change the course of many generations to come, while buried in mystery.

Chapter 6

Bois Marchant

Bêti loved a good cemetery.

It always appeared as under looked architecture to her. Many names end up here, on headstones, without the hope of being read or remembered.

Yet, a cemetery was just that, no-one needing to forget the loved one who left this mortal abode.

She felt a rush of excitement as she turned off the road and through the black wrought iron gates, thrilled to find there might actually be a cemetery to search, after weeks of mounting frustration. The information had come in a chance encounter at the Council Tax office, chatting to the clerk.

"Family history? Me too, I love it! I've managed to find ten generations. Mind you, some of them turned out to be a bit unsavoury. Esclaves* Marrons, Lascars pickèrs ratifs*, coolies, my poor Nani couldn't stand the shock, she died 3 months after knowing the truth. A devout Sunni musulman, can you believe it? Where did yours live?"

"I don't really know," Bêti had replied. "I've tracked back to 181 on the census records, but I can't find out any real detail on where they lived or what they did. How did you find out about the unsavoury bits?"

"Oh, mainly through their professions and where they lived and where they died. A couple of mine died in the workhouse. My family migrated to la rue Ail Doré in Plaine Verte after the 'bagarre raciale.'* Have you checked the municipal cemetery's register?"

"There's a register at the cemetery?"

The hedges that separated the cemetery from the main road around Bois Marchant into the town centre had grown high, so drivers speeding by on the highway

---

* Esclaves - slaves
* pickèrs ratifs – Muslim Shia body flagellation and piercing by skewers
* bagarre raciale – racial unrest

would never know it was there. The clerk had told her that when it was opened as a new municipal facility in 1883 it had been a well-known landmark but had filled up its allotted space by the 1960s.

The tarmacked car parking area had six spaces, all empty. Heavily reddened by the iron rich soil characteristic of this part of the island, the car park was bordered by the warden's abandoned cottage, a whitewashed chapel, and a low stone wall.

Beyond the chapel lay an acre of headstones sloping down towards a dead and dried sugar cane field.

Bêti felt a slight shiver as she got out of the car. It was cold for May, at the end of what had been a disappointingly late winter.

There weren't many blossoms, or early summer flowers.

Although it was mid-morning, the lingering dew from the previous night floated low across grass around the graves, the sky a deep cerulean expanse through which a pale sun fleetingly appeared. This was not a usual scene in the suburbs of the capital.

Even for a graveyard it was quiet.

Beti headed for the chapel to search for clues. 'Whatever is lurking out there, I am here to find you!' she thought wryly as she prepared to hunt down the past. Woman on a mission.

She could see that the chapel was boarded up and the smaller windows high up were broken by stone-shaped holes. She peered hopefully through a gap in the boarding, but the chapel had been stripped bare, not even the altar remained. On the front porch at the top of the arch, 1883 was carved into the stone. Dead end, she thought, liking her pun. She could see that many of the graves were sinking and overgrown. More than half of the ornate headstones in this top area lean precariously, as if they might keel over at any moment. Some were laid flat.

A footpath dissected the rows of graves, connecting the border where the Chinese graves started. The grass was overgrown, weeds roamed freely across the ground and the atmosphere spoke to Bêti of forgetfulness and neglect.

She followed the path around the outside of the chapel and began to look at the headstones to get her bearings. The first burials had been closest to the chapel and dated from 1883. They stood in the shade of an acacia tree close to the back of the chapel. They looked small, probably the children's section. She'd start close and work her way along the rows out towards the far wall. Her main problem was going to make herself concentrate on who she was looking for and not get distracted. Bêti knew she might be looking for more than one grave but hoped she would find everyone she was searching for in one plot. She needed to know where to look.

She continued to walk up and down the rows of graves, picking her way gingerly over the wet grass and taking care to avoid 'stepping' on the dead. She became distracted by the names, dates and details she found. She was unable to stop herself from reading the information carved into stone. Most of the graves had traditional French names: Robillard, Pierre, Monge, Evarette. She hurried, giving each gravestone a quick once over. This was just her first visit anyway. It would be a miracle if she found what she was searching for, the first time. A couple more rows then she'd have to leave it. Rushing along a final row she stumbled a few times over the uneven ground and, as she stepped over a fallen headstone, she caught her foot and tripped on some creepers that had run across the ground from a particularly ornate grave. Now on her hands and knees she glanced at the stone in front of her and – this was it!

A beautiful but overgrown pale stone, tall and pointed with elegant, smooth, rounded dark green marble columns at each side. The wording, elaborately carved, was reasonably clear, although overgrown by poison ivy.

Maude De La Tour, beloved wife of ... Died 4 May 1768 at Pointe des Lascars. She tried to remove the creeping grass covering the next line, but it clung tenaciously. At the bottom she could just make out, ...and, devoted husband Mohan, died tragically & Cremated on 21st November 1768.

Bêti leapt up, elated at having succeeded, and desperate to clean the stone further to find the full details. Then she realised that she was going to be late. "I'll be back," she said to the headstone, then felt foolish that she had spoken out loud. She ran back on the path and around the chapel to her car.

'What tragedy?' Bêti thought aloud, then realising she was on her own, she looked around and saw no one at any other graves. She was right, there has been a mixed class union, a coolie and a white. A poor and a rich. An indentured worker and an owner. Heaven and earth. A spot like that in a lineage had to be wiped out. At least in the records. Whoever engraved this epitaph must have done so much later when the island became free from colonial powers. Someone would have known the couple closely, to have bothered erecting this tombstone.

The clerk she met had given her a golden nugget of information. It was right that the municipal cemetery's register recorded everyone who became tenants at the Bois Marchant facility.

Fortunately, she could re-run her grandmother's birthplace as recorded and found out that her mother's birth certificate had a 'no calling' on her records too. Place, date, name was enough to guess a deliberate erasure of a name. It could only have been of a white family who couldn't afford to soil their name. Someone who eloped. Someone who left the white family for a subaltern. It was obvious!

When Bêti traced back the sugar estates around Pointe des Lascars, she found only one in the region. One family who owned most of the North-eastern part of the island. The De La Tour - the same family who was mentioned in Bernardin de Saint Pierre's Paul et Virginie, a short novel about innocent love. Paul et Virginie, the story of two island children whose love for each other, begun in their infancy, thrives in an unspoiled natural setting but ends tragically when civilization interferes. Bernardin was posted in 1768 to its colony of Île de France (Mauritius).

His sea journey was perilous, marked by death and scurvy. On the island he was appalled by aspects of the French administration. He was shocked by the treatment of slaves on plantations. Despite having family members engaged in the maritime slave trade, he attacked the brutality of slavery in his correspondence and subsequent publications.

*In the weeks that followed she searched library archives and genealogy files. At first it had been easy, working back through her parents' birth certificates, then census records. She had got back to her great-grandmother, in 1921, when she had been eight years old and living with her grandparents. Despite many hours of research and investigation she was stuck and couldn't discover what had happened to her parents. She had first come across her grandmother, Rani, on her mother's birth certificate.

The light was fading. The trees on top of Signal mountain grew steadily darker and spread shadows down towards the harbour, where the motionless water had darkened to resemble black syrup. The few rows of houses in the distance shone lights against the deep blue, almost purple, sky. As she drank her rum, laced with ice and water, Bêti pieced together everything that she had found out, trying to reassure herself with a logical explanation. The day had been long and zoomed across generations of history to reveal her own mother's sad and unfortunate childhood. She took a gulp of the drink and a long-suppressed fear welled up, and with it an old anxiety that death was not the end of a straight line. And there was something else, some nagging feeling that she thought she recognised but couldn't put a name to. She had felt it a few times since her investigations had begun and she didn't like it. It felt unsafe. How she missed her Maa tonight but also relieved she wasn't there.

What could she have told her about her findings?

She had been so caught up in her thoughts that she hadn't noticed the first stars shining brightly up above. All she could see now was the outline of the long mountain ridge against the last fading westerly light. This window seemed to have been designed especially for quiet contemplation of the view, with its changing colours throughout the day, season by season. She caught the reflection of herself in the mirror under the candlelight, and she wondered which part of her face looked like the elusive great great grandmother she had been searching for, making it look like a riddle set by a sphinx to decipher.

Going back to the archives the next day was all way too natural to do. Bêti now had a name to search for, one which could lead her towards a main key opening locked doors, long forgotten by history.

Her footsteps echoed on the concrete floor as she made her way along the furthest corridor towards the windowless archives room. There were few people in the research room, and the ambiance was the usual calm hush. She smiled at the archivist as she signed in.

"Hello. Me again!" the archivist smiled back. "I've found something that might help you. It's the right area, anyway."

They had gotten to know each other a little. When she first arrived Bêti had little idea where to start. Despite her habitual placid look-like-being-efficient public servant's demeanour, Reshmi, the archivist had proved to be helpful, listening to Beti's story and suggesting various documents that might help in her search for information on her elusive parentage.

Bêti was thrilled when she was handed a pile of church registers from the parishes.

Each was a leather-bound volume, around two feet high and held together with frayed black ribbon.

She was amazed at the excitement she felt in being allowed to handle these historical documents.

Before opening them she reverently brushed her fingers over the hard leather covers, imagining the hands that had first touched them, the clerks and scribes of the parish, a cut above the common herd, and relatively affluent because they could both read and write.

'Since you told me about the possibility of having a white lineage, I asked around, and someone told me I could ask for the St Louis Cathedral's parish. It used to act like a headquarters for the island's small parishes.

If one is not an indentured worker, then other inhabitants would mostly be Christians and all of them would be recorded in these registers. This includes all births, marriages, christenings and funerals. I thought you might want to take a look, just in case something rang a bell.' Reshmi finished with a smile.

'That's fabulous, thank you so much! I indeed have a precise name to search for today.'

'Really?' What is it?' Reshmi was genuinely interested and gave Bêti one of her raised pencilled eyebrows looks.

The first volume Bêti opened was covering the births in that area from 1722 to 1767.

Inventaire des registres paroissiaux de l'Ile de France (Ile Maurice): Compagnie des Indes, 1722-1767

Each event had been carefully entered in a beautiful copperplate hand, registering the names of the parents and the child, and the date of baptism. In some cases, the names of godparents were also recorded. The paper on which the names were inscribed was a kind of parchment, Bêti guessed, heavy and rough, the colour faded to grey, but still with thick black ink, legible after nearly three hundred years. She went painstakingly through the lists of names, checking each one carefully, but not finding De La Tour.

One of the most surprising discoveries was the number of births recorded as "base" or even "bastard."

Her notion of the nineteenth century had been of an era of great propriety and strict morality.

Evidently, this was not the full story, particularly among the lower classes, as many of the people in the register seemed to be agricultural labourers, jobbing tradesmen, or servants.

However, no 'batard' was in the records next to the De La Tours. Or deliberately wiped out?

Bêti felt a taste of ash in her mouth. So much cruelty and prejudice have probably run down her bloodline, she would never discover the truth, as it happened.

Such was the harshness of the colonial system when men decided to give in to their bloated greed and use human beings as mere commodities.

Chapter 7

जहाझिया – Ship Passengers

"Between the seventeenth and mid-nineteenth centuries, the continuities and connections between free and unfree labour prevailed over clear-cut opposition such as those between wage earners and serfs, indentured immigrants and servants, in both time and space. Imperial, national, regional, and local features must be taken into consideration in order to understand how the whole system worked.

Thus, the French case is of interest, not because it was the land of Colbert's as opposed to liberal England, or because nineteenth-century France was the country of free, codified law compared with Germany, which still lagged behind. On the contrary, France is of interest because the galley system projected its main features well into the eighteenth century and was transmuted into forms of forced recruitment both in

France and in the Indian Ocean. This case is all the more likely to raise new questions as, contrary to a popular misconception, common law in England was in fact accompanied by a considerable degree of regulation and state intervention and labour remained subject to criminal constraints until the end of the nineteenth century.

The masters and servants' rules were not only enforced in Britain; they strongly influenced post slavery labour in its colonies, while the navy continued to use coercion on Britons as well as on colonial subjects.

These interactions took place in addition to more general ones with India in terms of institutions and labour.

While British norms and perceptions translated into various forms of bondage and slavery in India, and thereby helped perpetuate slavery well after its official abolition, the latter nevertheless predated any British intervention.

The solution adopted in India and the practices that were accepted did not result solely from British influences, but rather from interaction between those influences and local labour relations and values.

Mauritius and Reunion Island seem to confirm the importance of the Atlantic paradigm, particularly the domination exerted by European powers, the dissemination of the plantation system, and its heritage in post slavery forms of immigration and labour.

But despite the existence of plantations, experiences in Mauritius and Reunion Island differed from those in the Atlantic in many areas—the forms of labour recruitment, the organization of labour, the role of Arab, Indian, Swahili elites, and its final outcome. Although there were differences between the plantation systems in the Indian Ocean and the Atlantic, those were even greater for other forms of labour, farming, and bondage. This has several implications from the standpoint of dynamics.

While labour markets in the North Atlantic were homogenous in terms of wages and forms of labour, such homogeneity never developed in the Indian Ocean. Thus, instead of a successive shift from slavery to indenture to wage labour, multiple forms of dependence coexisted over time.

Consequently, standardized labour and production could not be imposed in the Indian Ocean World as they would in the North-Atlantic world. On the contrary, major developments took place before and after the golden era of centralization and standardization (1870–1980). Western hegemony chiefly benefited from this process, whereas the Indian Ocean development was primarily linked to different forms of production and labour such as continuing labour-intensive growth and, along with it, persistent forms of bondage that were perfectly compatible with capitalism.

Trade has probably been the most thoroughly explored topic in history and social science research in the Indian Ocean. Trade and trade networks crossed imperial and ecological boundaries. Some historians have identified three main periods: long-distance trade prior to the seventeenth century; imperial conquest in two centuries that followed; and mass migration after that.

Trade flourished in the Indian Ocean in ancient times; there is evidence of trade down the Red Sea and, on the African side, as early as 5000 BCE. During the first millennium BCE, connections were developed with the Mediterranean and between India, Africa, and China. With the growth of Islam, beginning in the ninth century, trade in the Indian Ocean expanded significantly. Arabs had long traded with the Indian coast and Indians. When Arabs became Muslims, they continued to trade, and conversions took place very early along the Indian coastline. Islam began making converts in Southeast Asia in the late thirteenth century.

From Kerala, Islam flowed on to Southeast Asia. Extensive trade with China was handled by Chinese and Gujarat merchants.

In the fifteenth century and later, most Asian spices were consumed by Asians.

India alone consumed twice as many fine spices as the whole of Europe. Porcelain, metals, ivory, rice, and slaves were the most important items of trade.

During this period, the leading port cities included Sofala in the far south of East Africa, which provided gold and ivory from the interior.

To the north, Kilwa* was the principal emporium between 1250 and 1330. By 1500 the largest port city was Mombasa, a prosperous centre of trade in ivory and gold from the south for manufactures in the west and north. Aden was a powerful port city owing to its location at the entrance to the Red Sea, while the sizable ports of Gujarat were certainly prominent centres of exchange.

In this period, the main port was Cambay.

On the Malabar Coast, Calicut was the dominant port. The Portuguese helped militarize Indian Ocean trade, but they failed to fundamentally transform its nature or patterns in the western part of the region. Instead they superimposed their activities on the pre-existing trade structure. Mozambique became the vital link in the chain between Goa and Lisbon. The Portuguese

---

* Kilwa – a region in the Lindi region of South Tanzania, today a UNESCO World Heritage site.

system was a vast protection racket, for the Portuguese were selling protection from violence they themselves had created. In the middle of the seventeenth century, Portuguese control ran up against challenges from the Omanis, the Dutch, and the British.

Like the Portuguese, the Dutch sought to control the spice trade. Cinnamon, cloves, nutmeg, and mace made up the famous four spices of the Dutch East India Company. The Dutch also made widespread use of slaves to produce these items.

However, this proved more difficult with spices than with sugar. Pepper was the main product; it was cultivated in several areas, not all of them controlled by the Dutch.

Thus, at least in Malabar, the Dutch were confronted by the same problems that had hindered Portuguese efforts: the production area was inland, whereas European power was effective only on the coast and at sea.

The Portuguese were expelled from Muscat and an aggressive new Omani dynasty emerged.

They built an empire, but its reach was limited to East Africa. After 1750, Britain, and to a lesser extent France, took the lead in the western Indian Ocean. Shipbuilding contributed to these dynamics, and the SE Trade winds from subtropical areas below the Tropic of Capricorn eased navigation.

Weaker monsoons in the northern part of the Indian Ocean were accompanied by a larger number of more powerful cyclones in the southern region. Overall, the ocean around Mascarene Islands (Mauritius, Reunion, Rodrigues) provided a calm haven for the seafarers and the British and French tradesmen.

Shipbuilding is seldom independent of the geographical environment in which the ships are used; it is also highly adaptive and mobile.

In Europe, two basic types of ship, the galley and the round ship, served as models for later development. From the sixteenth to the early nineteenth century, gradual innovations continued, but no radically new ship appeared until the invention of the steam engine.

In the Indian Ocean, there were marked differences in the shape and design of hulls from one coastal area to another, and even within a single trading region there were highly specialized craft considered suitable only for particular kinds of water and sailing conditions. The multitude of vessels can be divided into three main categories. In the western half, as far as Bengal, shipbuilding followed an Indo-Islamic tradition and produced a number of common hull shapes.

The term 'dhow' was used by westerners for a variety of craft, large and small, which dominated the western part of the Indian Ocean, for centuries. Teak from Malabar, which was highly resistant to decay, was used to make a hull following the carvel method: the planks of the hull were laid edge to edge rather than overlapping as in Western ships. They were held together by coir ropes stitching that passed through holes in the planks. The hulls could carry heavy cargo, camels, horses, and even elephants. The ships were rigged with the famous triangular sails known as "lateen".

This type of sail probably developed independently in several places, even if the Arab influence appears to have been decisive. The 'prahu' and the bamboo 'sampan' became predominant in the Indonesian islands, Malaya and Burma.

These were fast, light boats, mostly used for inland seas. The Chinese junk, on the other hand, was the high seas vessel par excellence.

In the earlier centuries of Islamic expansion toward India and Indonesia, the shipbuilders of the Persian Gulf and the Red Sea upgraded their undecked smaller craft into bigger vessels.

During the sixteenth century, the Gujarat Sultanate and the Moplas of Malabar manufactured ships weighing about 150 tons each. They were made of wood with iron nails. In the seventeenth century, the crews of Malabar ships were equipped with stinkpots (a type of primitive hand grenade) and lances but lacked onboard artillery. In Calicut, the caste known as Odayis specialized in building ships of about 350–400 tons.

It is a well-known fact that the Portuguese exported the maritime revolution to the Indian Ocean. European ships proved to be superior to all other vessels in the Indian Ocean, at least on the high seas. At the same time, many of these great Portuguese ships were made in Asia. Due to cheaper labour and materials, the cost per ton in India was only half what it was in Europe. Caulking in particular was very expensive and in any case this technique had no advantage over the cheaper traditional north Indian method of rabbeting. Indian ships continued to use coir cables and cordage rather than hemp ropes, but coir was perfectly adequate as long as it remained in salt-water to keep it strong. European supremacy was thus limited to the high seas. Along the coasts, as in the Mediterranean, the superiority of the round ship in no way threatened the existence of other boats, including galleys, which had the advantages of speed and manoeuvrability. In northern India, gunpowder weaponry for riverine warfare was introduced by the

Mughals. They used small boats known as khelna to record the river depth before the main fleet moved in. In 1582, the Mughals hired Portuguese sailors for the Mughal Eastern Fleet stationed at Dacca.

The Mughals decided not to adopt all the European innovations, as local boats retained their importance in both war and coastal trading activities. As a result, the Mughals confined most of their maritime attention to the coasts of Gujarat and Bengal.

Outside the ports, the Mughals delegated the protection of their maritime route either to the trading communities themselves or to the specialized Abyssinian corsairs of Janjira on the western coast.

Toward the end of the seventeenth century, the Sidis of Janjira became a powerful non-state naval power in the Konkan region.

The Hindu artisans called Sutars in the Konkan region were involved in shipbuilding. The Sidis engaged in naval conflict with the Marathas. Their largest ships weighed between 300 and 400 tons; they were thus unfit to fight European ships but could face the Ottoman vessels in the Arabian Sea.

Indeed, the Ottoman ships were slow and difficult to manoeuvre; they were also weak and most of the sailors were inexperienced labourers.

In Bengal, the situation was different.

To gain control of this area, the Mughals needed to outfit an enormous fleet of riverboats. Furthermore, the local Rajput Zamindars were well equipped with guns and well served by European gunners and sailors.

During much of the monsoon, when the Mughal army was forced to endure a long period of waiting, these Zamindar navies were quite capable of engaging in military operations.

Copper, coins, rice, bhang (hemp), and opium were distributed to sailors as incentives for their efforts. In Mughal India, a large ship had several categories of crew: the nakhuda* owned the ship and determined the itinerary; the mu'allim* was the captain; then came the chief of the sailors, then storekeepers,

---

* nakhuda – Captain in Persian
* mu'allim – teacher in Arabic, but here also the captain

pursers, gunners, look-outs, and common seamen. In every major port such as Hormuz, Aden, Cambay, Surat, and Malacca, as the shipping season drew near, a crowd of sailors, pilots, and captains gathered to offer their services. The first Europeans to enter the Indian Ocean, like Vasco de Gama in 1498, employed Indian pilots from Gujarat to set their course.

The Maratha navy was built between 1657 and 1659 to fight the Sidis, who were allied with the Mughals. The Marathas employed Muslim sailors as well as Dutch seamen for their superior technical skills.

By 1600, Indians ships had already reached the same ratio as European vessels of about one man for every four tons of cargo.

By the late seventeenth century, the shipbuilders of the Coromandel Coast had thoroughly mastered the technique of European naval construction.

It was a fact that ships built in the Indian Ocean were not used more extensively for Atlantic voyages due to political opposition from shipping interests in Europe, which feared competition.

The monsoon, a strait jacket for millennia, now became largely irrelevant when confronted by steam ships. This process definitely changed maritime work and labour relationships. Prior to that same date, British vessels gradually gained supremacy in terms of strength, solidity, and swiftness over their rivals around the world, particularly in the Indian Ocean."

Bêti shifts herself on the rattan armchair.

Long hours of reading made her start to piece together historical facts, notes from records in the archives and registers with her own discovery, projecting a certain possibility of truth to herself.

Tonight, she feels her bigarade tisane feel sweeter than previously, maybe she is bringing closer that formidable cane to herself, one that built the island's economy from sweat and blood of her ancestors.

She is appreciative of this granulated mass she often takes for granted.

The next day, Bêti took a drive to explore Pointe des Lascars.

It is a fine sunny day with a blue sky and small puffs of cloud scattered here and there.

Between sky, land and sea, the coastal landscape that it closes, is just breath-taking. Although development is precarious, with very few social and sports activities for young and old, the place stands out for the authenticity it exudes. The stretch of the beach is almost empty of any bathers or picnic buffs, apart from fishermen.

Bêti admires the stretch of emerald and ultramarine stretch of the sea with soft white sands. She tries to think about what could have been the life of a fisherman living in colonial times.

Could Mohan S., the name she saw engraved on the tombstone, have been a fisherman?

Her research brought her here and discovering that some of the indentured workers joined the local ex-slaves who converted themselves to live off the sea when they ran away from their masters. Fishing brought food and bonding with the previous workers of the sugar estates.

A breeze from the lagoon blew Beti's hair and she wondered what lurked under that magnificent expanse of water.

The world of the reef, seen from the inside, is quite different from how it appears on the screen of a TV or picture. At first sight it can seem like an idyllic place, full of amazing creatures that glide gracefully among the branches of coral with no apparent purpose apart from that of being admired. In reality the reef is a world dominated by fear. Those colours which seem so beautiful to us exist only as a function of the struggle for life or death that never ceases for an instant. The colourful liveries serve to attract prey, or to confuse predators, or even as warning signals, as in the case of the butterfly fish which swim quite nonchalantly out in the open because the strident colours of their bodies and fins tell everyone, in the code of the reef, that they are in fact quite poisonous. Then every underwater crevice hides an animal ambush. Perfectly camouflaged octopus peep out of clefts in the rocks, their tentacles drawn in under their bodies, ready to twist around the first creature that comes too close.

Moray eels spend their lives waiting in ambush with their yellow bodies hidden in their lairs with just their heads sticking out of the opening.

Even the multi-coloured sea anemones, which wave about in the currents like flowers in the wind, are not what they seem; they have stinging tentacles that can paralyze with a single touch.

Finally, there are the big predators, like the barracuda which move around in groups of hundreds and attack all together, or the giant carnivorous groupers with mouths bigger than a man's head, and the sharks which patrol the seabed with an air of having nothing to fear. In this cruel, beautiful, alien world every living being spends its life balanced between the search for smaller animals to capture and the fear of being devoured in its turn by the bigger ones.

Not dissimilar to how it is on land.

Survival is key. Faced with adversity of an enslaved state must have been even worse to many during those colonial times.

Bêti is startled by a rustle coming from the tall casuarina trees and stands still, to listen.

She imagines that probably in early times, there would have been monkeys (macaques) around introduced by the French.

'You mustn't try to befriend or feed macaques', people would say. If you feed them, they think you are subordinate. It means they think you are lower than they are.

Nobody wants to be less important, do they?

Yet this is what made the fabric of this often island called 'paradise'.

Chapter 8
The St Géran

One night I'll break free,

and hair streaming behind

I'll race for the beach.

The wind, brackish and thick,

will soften the air and cling to my cheek.

I won't be able to hear you

over the sound of my feet pounding

the wood,

the roar of the water,

the hot lure of sand.

Around me the sea-brush will twist and sing,

sheltering the boardwalk in a thousand arches:

a tunnel of green that will carry me

away back to the sea.

Reaching Poudre D'Or, Bêti looked again at the monument erected in memory of the wreck of St Géran, facing the waves crashing on the black pillowed basalt rocks which were amassed here some millions of years ago when the island was formed out of a massive eruption.

It was a very crude and simple concrete and stone structure, which didn't say much of the huge tragedy that befell it on this stunning coast.

The most famous ship name in the history of Mauritius is the slave ship St. Géran which, whilst bringing colonists, was shipwrecked in 1744 on a fringing reef off the island's northeast coast.

St Géran, with 110 crew and colonists aboard and cargo of iron sugar cauldrons, went aground and broke up on the reef at night, 17 August 1744.

Falling masts crashed onto the boats before launching.

Makeshift rafts capsized. Only 9 survived.

The incident provided the basis for 1750's best seller in Europe, Paul et Virginie by Bernardin de St. Pierre.

The tales of shipwrecks, of vessels that lay on the bottom of the sea, pirates and filibusters which had hidden chests of gold coins and gems, inspired minds to dream of breathing underwater and finding treasure. Many had even endeavoured throughout their lives doing so.

Few had gone searching for the unmentioned slaves who died in those shipwrecks. Nor were there any of their names on the epitaphs or monuments.

Tales told have been passed on from generations to generations, and today the elders sitting under the boutique awnings influenced by a few shots of locally brewed rum and beer still recall those haunting words.

The beginning of the tale was always the same, but the stories of the ship's crew, passengers' and slaves' survival changed with the storyteller's moods—each different, but as poignant as the last.

Some survived by riding a whale to shore; others swam underwater and grew gills.

Occasionally, passengers were rescued by great flying albatrosses that swooped down and carried them home.

"The secrets are lost to the waves. Only the sea knows, and she keeps her secrets well. And maybe one day she will tell you."

The ship heaved again, rising almost vertically before falling to crash with an ominous crack of timbers. The man on the ladder lost his grip and fell heavily, landing on his shoulder. With a howl of pain, he grabbed his arm, now twisted grotesquely. The ship pitched sideways, and there were renewed cries from above decks.

A groan from overhead grew louder until the wall opposite Virginie's bunk suddenly caved in with a deafening explosion. She threw herself over a slave in distress to protect him.

When she opened her eyes, an enormous mast lay atop the bunks. She got only a momentary glance at the man's lifeless eyes staring skyward before water began gushing through the opening, filling the hold. Other people clambered and wriggled out of the bunks now submerged under the deluge. With the extra weight of the water coming in, the St Géran could no longer right herself and began to list heavily. Some of the people tumbled out of their bunks, linking arms as they scrambled for the ladder.

One young man wrenched a splintered board loose from where the mast had come through and used it to hammer the trapdoor until it burst upward. The climb up the ladder was precarious as more water cascaded through, beating on their heads, trying to bear them down, but down was certain death.

"Paul!" Her scream was lost in the storm.

She scrutinised the darkness in the hope that Paul would be there waiting for her and seeing the tragedy would come to rescue her. The broken mast had sailors trapped in its lines. They flailed helplessly, waves washing over them as they tried desperately to free themselves. One man, already dead, flopped flaccidly with the churning of the ocean, washed time and again by the great force of sweeping waves.

All around her, men shouted, women and children cried and clutched to one another. The ship rode lower as it took on more water. She thought she saw a starkly brown face bobbing in the waves beyond the boat. She hesitated a moment more and then stepped out onto the slippery deck, letting herself slither closer and closer to the edge.

Someone caught her wrist and shouted to remove her heavy dress and to jump overboard. But in a flash, she remembered Paul, she had promised herself to him, and her purity with was for him …!

When the next wave hit and took her with it, she wasn't prepared for the battering force of the water, driving her under. She fought her way toward the surface, but another wave crashed upon her, tumbling her through the water so that she didn't know which way was up. Her lungs were ready to burst when her head broke free into the air. She drew in a quick breath just before another wave pummelled her, crushing her with pulverizing force. Clawing at the water, she swam toward the surface, but the weight of her bulky dress was sodden.

'Hold my arm, shouted someone, it was an Indian man, trying to catch hold of her to save her from bobbing again under the waves. A chunk of wood slammed into her head, nearly knocking her unconscious. She grabbed at it, hauling herself partially onto it, and tried to clear her foggy vision. "Paul!" she cried. "Madame hold my h-...!"

Another wave washed over her, filling her mouth. Her stomach convulsed and she threw up all the salt-water she'd swallowed. Exhausted, she dragged herself further onto the wooden beam she desperately grasped. The man trying to rescue her had disappeared, she looked around for him and couldn't see him anymore.

In the distance, faint screams came to her through the raging storm, but she could no longer see the ship. The endless night seemed to stretch on, and she wondered vaguely if this was eternity, if she was in one of the places in hell, she was threatened with by the priest back home. Through the gloom, she thought she saw movement. She squinted into dark faces, bobbing on the water atop strange floating logs. They spoke words she didn't understand. Her eyes closed, but she dreamt that hands reached out of the darkness, dragging her. Mohan, who had witnessed St Géran in distress from the shore, had taken his boat like other fishermen in the rescue effort. He saw Virginie being washed as the young woman looked at the water engulfing the ship in violent throngs. He managed to swim to her and catch her hand.

Virginie remembered the pain as something wrenched her arm. Then the upward thrust of the wind blew her into the air, one second she was flying then lost in the thick foam of the crashing crests. The next moment she was plummeting, dead weight in the dark. Terror jolted through her. She drew breath to scream, only to feel the spank of the sea, like a wet fist of concrete between her shoulder blades, stinging even as it slowed her fall. She plunged beneath the waves, headfirst. A stronger wave hit both Mohan and Virginie, each plunging in the inky depth.

Then, it all stopped.

Mohan in a brave effort to rescue Virginie who lost the battle to the fierce sea.

The early hours of dawn brought a scene of desolation. Bodies washed up on the beach. Baptiste was sitting, lost in the distance, the body of his friend Mohan lying next to him.

The ancient Sanskrit epic of the Ramayana told of a time when Hanuman, the Indian monkey warrior-god, needed herbs to treat the wounded in his army during his battle against the demonic King Ravana* of Ceylon.

There were no medicinal herbs to be found there, so Hanuman went back to India and brought back a piece of the Himalayas where the plants he needed, grew, but he accidently dropped it on the island. This saved the life of Laxmana, Ram's younger brother who got fatally wounded by Ravana.

---

* King Ravana – nine headed king from the Ramayana who abducted Sita

The islanders swear by their local medicinal herbs which now grow abundantly everywhere.

Bêti picked some citronella grass to make an infusion. It is believed to bring relief to a sore throat while also calming the nerves. She has got used to natural herbs to treat anything mild, something she learnt from her Maman.

The trip to Pointe des Lascars and Plaine des Roches had been quite emotional. Beads of perspiration trickled down Beti's back, as the humidity was high. Not a leaf moved.

The air was still, even the birds were not singing.

The heaviness of the atmosphere increased the young woman's feeling of oppression since she had been imagining the wreck of the St Géran.

William Willoughby

For a big man his agility was astonishing and even at the age of forty he could beat any of his hands in a race to the top.

On his way to lunch in Plymouth, on a winter's day in 1796, William Willoughby heard that the Dutton Indiaman had gone aground nearby with 500 troops, women and children.

He raced to the scene, pulled himself out to the ship on a rope, and, finding panic, took charge by threatening to run through any man who did not obey him.
As boats came alongside, he supervised the evacuation of women and children, then the troops. All but fifteen lives were saved, and William cheered to the skies on coming ashore.

Among his most attractive qualities was a love of chivalry.

A French officer recorded how, on receiving a captain's sword in surrender, William drew his own with the words, 'Pray take this and keep it as a souvenir of the profound admiration with which your bravery has inspired me', before offering his arm to the wounded while conducting him to a cabin beside his own. More than once he provided for the dependents of those he had defeated. If he was the beau ideal of the navy commander, he also had a human side that included a strong streak of cupidity. He never forgot his humble origins and never missed an opportunity to enhance his fortune, pursuing prize money almost as avidly as he did glory. Nor was he politically innocent. He obtained a seat in Parliament and used his preference to secure promotion, as he wrote to a friend, 'I am much older now and can't get to the Mast Head as quick as I used to. I want to be an Admiral.'

Duly promoted, he was rewarded with the Indies command. That was in 1804, the year before Trafalgar, when he turned forty-seven. Four years on, he might have reflected sardonically on the transience of glory. While Nelson had won immortality in death, William had been left to fume in his tropical exile – constrained from prosecuting war at sea and undermined by political enemies at home. True, his piratical eye had brought him a phenomenal amount of prize money. India had made his fortune, to the tune of some £80,000 (about £5 million today).

However, William was above all a fighter, who had accepted his command 'in the hope of giving a blow to the inveterate and restless Enemies of Mankind'.

He had succeeded in so far as destroying a small Dutch squadron in Java. As for the most inveterate of those foes, he had failed to strike at the French. Worse, they had tarnished the reputation of which he was properly proud. The trouble was the so-called 'Gibraltar of the East', the twin islands of Ile de

France and Bourbon, or, as they are now known, Mauritius and Réunion.

It is hard today, looking at a map of the Indian Ocean and locating those tiny specks.

They lie due east of the vastness of Madagascar like pebbles in the shadow of a mountain – to imagine that at the time they appeared to threaten the East India Company's control of India, and consequently Britain's survival as a great power.

Quite simply, the benefits of Trafalgar had not been felt in the Eastern Seas.

'Here alone in the whole world', a naval historian has written, 'there were still French warships at sea in a good state of efficiency.'

Here alone, the French retained a capacity to strike at Britain's commercial lifeline, and in the past year they had done so from Ile de France with spectacular success – under William's nose.

On top of his problems, William had a devilishly elusive foe - Bonaparte. He now lacked the resources for fleet action; instead, Ile de France and Bourbon provided havens for navy captains and privateers who had no intention of giving battle but proved infuriatingly adept at picking off isolated merchantmen. An even greater threat, more effective than any frigate captain, was posed by one of the great corsairs. Robert Surcouf had made his name and fortune years before William's arrival in the East.

At the Emperor's urging, he returned to Ile de France in 1807 in Revenant, an 18-gun sloop built to Surcouf's design, her hull completely sheathed in copper, one of the fastest ships afloat. Over the past year, Revenant had become the bane of shipping in the Bay of Bengal, where she had taken more than thirty prizes. In one two-month spell alone, nineteen British vessels were captured by Revenant and two French frigates. The losses produced squeals of outrage from the merchants of Calcutta who drafted a memorial to the Admiralty, pointing out that 'the two small islands of Mauritius and Bourbon' were the source of their 'unprecedented suffering', and laying responsibility directly at William's door. Surcouf's activity had been conducted 'within one hundred leagues of Madras roads, the principal Station of His

Majesty's ships, where at the same time the Flag of a British Rear-Admiral was displayed.'

William was bitter, and with good reason. Finding a handful of French raiders in the vastness of the Indian Ocean was an impossible task. Moreover, although the merchants' losses were indeed severe, they failed to mention that he had offered convoys to their ships and they had declined. It suited the nature of Calcutta's trade to engage small local vessels, or country ships, for individual voyages rather than wait for convoys to be assembled – even though this exposed them to predators. The Bombay merchants, who accepted William's offer, had not lost a ship. Nor had any Indiamen been taken, thanks to the convoy system.

'The merchants of Bengal', he wrote angrily, 'have made individual interest in their study, and not the general good.'

Nothing would have pleased William more. Two years earlier he had presented a plan for a joint Navy and Army invasion, starting with the seizure of Bourbon and followed by a landing on the southern shore of Ile de France. It was the one blow that he could deal to the enemy.

Logistically, it was ambitious but, with the Company's forces in India, feasible. Strategically, it was common sense.

The French had lost their last foothold in India with the capture of Pondicherry five years earlier. Seizing Ile de France and Bourbon would drive them from the Indian Ocean once and for all.

It was not simply a matter of securing British shipping. Bonaparte, it was known, still nurtured ambitions to supplant Britain in India.

In 1806 British forces recaptured the Cape from the Dutch and based a squadron to secure the route to India. But its impact had been limited.

A blockade of the islands, instituted recently in the hope of starving them into submission, had had little discernible impact; and it had not prevented ships slipping out on raiding expeditions.

In 1810, William entered Grand Port, the port to Île de France. A fierce battle followed, crushing the

British fleet who didn't know the treacherous reefs of
the port.

The French took advantage of their knowledge of Île
de la Passe. But their coming defeat in the next battle
still resounds with disbelief in the French psyche.
They want to believe that the island still belongs to
them.

Chapter 9

When Bêti first saw the beauty of the island after many years of absence, in her mind she thought time had warped her perception over modernity sprawling grotesquely, everywhere. An awed silence descended as she gaped at the exotic splendour in front of her. It was like a colourful mystical land that burst from the quivering liquidated earth, inviting and magical. If it had been described to her time and again by people not born on the island; they would call it paradise. The beaches of powdered white sand in the middle of a clear emerald and turquoise sea, and trees bearing fruit with as many colours as the rainbow. She remembered her surprise at how sweet and succulent the watermelons were. The warm sun and trees that stretched to the clouds on long stems astonished her. So did the tall breadfruit tree with its football sized green fruits. She remembered how she was fond of fritters her Maman made after a cyclone had battered the island. Breadfruit would scatter the ground, left to rot. It's blandness and being called a poor man's food, did not appeal to many people. They preferred what the boutique sinois* sold. Canned Pilchards in tomato sauce, sardines from Morocco, Watsonia corned mutton from Australia and frozen capitaine fish. So many years have shaped this island nation into a maze of cultures, cuisine and lore.

Beti thinks only of her Maman like many, who share the same past of their roots forgotten and lost. She was a stoic, hardworking, simple woman. She did not share her awful sadness that afflicts her at night, for the lack of bestowing her hard days to a kind ear she could call maa, of a brother or a sisterly hug.

There was none in her life.

Bêti thinks sadness is more prevalent among the islanders. She closes her eyes against the memory of that most unspeakable act of treachery. Slavery and indenture. There is only the sound of the birds breaking the silence.

------

* sinois – Chinese in French creole

Only nature pervades with wisdom and moves on.

As if nothing ever happened.

With the next trip to the archives, Bêti finished with a pair of dhal puri* and a couple of napolitaines*, sat on the top of Baie du Tombeau which gave a spectacular vista. The place was quiet, interspersed by a car stopping every now and then and some people coming out to take in the view but not staying for long.

Bêti ate her favourite street food of the island and the napolitaines which reminded her so much of her childhood. The sweet morsels of vanilla short biscuits and pink icing were decadent, and she heaved a huge sigh, while relishing them. The sun turned the horizon coral pink, and before her eyes, the sea slowly moved from deep flame orange, to fluttered light grey with ribbons of the remnants of the sunset colours. The offshore current was slightly choppy, breaking the

---

* dhal puri – thin dal savoury flatbread served with curries, popular street food in Mauritius

* napolitaines – sweet sandwiched butter biscuits with icing on top, popular pastry in Mauritius

surface into ripples, and she took a breath of the sea air with a sense of pleasure. Its ever-changing, elemental nature had always appealed to her. The hues and tones of the sea drew her like a magnet and made her stare for hours at a constant line of the horizon, hoping she would see something. It never happened. The horizon was one strange straight line which never altered, no matter what happened elsewhere.

Bêti scanned the list of all the indentured workers and their families from the sugar estate of Pointe des Lascars. There should be at least a record of a tragedy and loss of some of them, if the pointers, as she has been thinking, were the shipwreck of St Géran. The unexamined sources form a composite portrait of the island's colonial life which should have encompassed: passenger lists, estate inventories, tax lists, war compensation claims, early censuses, militia lists, parish records, land warrants, customs ledgers, and plantation records. Many such records did not exist. Almost all colonial historians of De La

Tour's generation were schooled in analysing literary sources, mostly penned by the uppermost members of society, and this made social history research frustrating, eye-straining, and often inconclusive, as Bêti is slowly discovering .... but also intriguing and exhilarating.

Like moths drawn to a flame, the early social historians and researchers who were present before her, were seeking illumination but risking incineration.

One thing was sure, the equation didn't add up. Or maybe, some runaways, should have been recorded. At least she would have some names to work with toward her quest. There should be some anomaly somewhere.

The vast estate of the De la Tour family was very well detailed in inked cursive letters. There were some non-Indian names, probably the slaves, and a long list of what looked like indentured workers who belonged to their sugarcane fields. This was a gold mine. She went through all the names and noticed many familiar ones still prevalent on the island. It was obvious that they were either wrongly spelled or intentionally written this way to simplify pronunciation.

When, after the enslaved were emancipated in the 1830s, the British began to rustle up replacement workers for plantations worldwide, this was the epithet they used for the indentured laborers they enlisted.

Ultimately, over the course of eight decades, they ferried more than a million "coolies" to more than a dozen colonies across the globe, including British Guiana, Trinidad, Jamaica, Suriname, Mauritius and Fiji. These were the first group of Indians abroad in any significant numbers, the vanguard of a larger, broader diaspora that India presently views with pride, courts and cultivates, but who were denigrated at the time. Coming from the lips of plantation managers and overseers, the coolie stung, a reminder of lowliness in the hierarchy of a sugar estate, a hierarchy based on race.

The British found it convenient to call every of their servants' 'coolie', preceding their first encounter with the word when they arrived in India. The coolie in its right place was used for porters, and also had an adage of 'what is paid for, i.e. a fee'.

Indians were at the bottom, below the English, the French and as well as the African slaves, sometimes assigned as "drivers," or foremen in charge of work gangs because of their longer experience. Each group held power over indentured labourers in the field and the factory, and each addressed their underlings as coolies. All castes among the indentured workers were merged together, some noted some omitted. Many later seized this opportunity to claim to be descended from a higher caste.

As such, most of them came from extremely poor and backward villages and hamlets where Brahmins and other higher castes were very few in number.

However, in current times in the Hindu community, which makes the majority population, many have earmarked their caste with precision and adhere to it. Bêti remembers the only link which existed between the land of origin of the indentured immigrants, India, to be analogous to Bollywood.

She knows what most of the Hindi words she had picked up from film songs meant.

She had heard them all intoned on screen so many times, melodramatically cueing violins, that they were part of the airtight space of her complicated ethnicity, having sensibility without sense.

Intuitively she knew, without much of her basic Hindi vocabulary from school stumbling ...words like: *Pyar, zindagi, jhootey, bachaao, shahdi, mushkil, akela, gunda, bhagwan* - love, life, liar, save me, wedding, trouble, alone, bandit, god.

And the most common reason when the heroine in distress tries to kill herself, either she's been rejected by her husband, or pregnant out of wedlock. Besides high drama, there were loads of soulful songs and pretty looking damsels.

While in her Bollywood thoughts, one name caught her attention in the register: Maude De la Tour. She saw it in the beginning and then it disappeared. She flipped the pages again and searched for the name and date.

The De la Tour family had 6 members residing on the island, but 22 of them in France, who came regularly. Maude went to France at the age of 13 and back when she was 18, after two years of regular listing of the De la Tour family, she suddenly disappears!

A year after her disappearance, the St Géran wreckage at Île d'Ambre is recorded.

Bêti felt her heart racing, her cheeks in flame, she went through the list of the indentured workers. Many are recorded as deceased; among them one particular name looks to have been erased. There was a blank space there with a greyish blotch.

Bêti counts the names again to find which one was erased, and what she sees was enough to make her gasp. 'Mohan' is the same she saw on the epitaph at the cemetery.

Could she be piecing the bits to that big elusive puzzle, right now? She stops to breathe properly again.

That possibility can't be true.

All along she had a doubt, but she couldn't have been so right. How to confirm it?

She closes the register, picks her things and walks out of the room waving a quick goodbye to the affable archivist, today all dressed in red and pink.

'It's Durga puja, married women dress in mata's colours' she had replied when Bêti had greeted and complimented her.

The clamour outside, and the bright daylight throws Bêti in a state of confusion. She felt as if she had been suddenly pushed into a different world.

She had hope in heart.

How she wished her Maman was alive, she would have flung into her arms and given her all the comfort she could to erase her long years of yearning.

Tears trickled down her cheeks, she was only aware of them when they reached the corner of her mouth in their bitter salinity. Her eyes blurred and she had to stop to find some tissue to sponge her tears. She grabbed her strength and headed to the direction of the Marchand de confits.

Some prickly salty sweet pickled fruits were all she needed right now. They were her pick-me-up comfort foods of all time.

Port Louis was as hot, streets as crowded as ever, with people moving briskly in a single flow like a giant caterpillar.

It felt rejuvenating.

In a way to say that life goes on when one enjoys little things in life.

Chapter 10

'Why should we build our happiness on the opinions of others, when we can find it in our own hearts?'
Jean-Jacques Rousseau

The cyclone has been battling hard since sunset.

The wind was rattling the shutters, catching the baby's mobile which Maude had made out of sugar straws. They swung and jumped and clashed in a mad Indian like dance. The strings would get all muddled and Maude knew she and Mohan would have to untwist them in the morning. The smell of rain filled the dark room, reaching up to the windows of the house, rising up from the damp earth, full of bruised frangipani blooms and dead leaves and small branches of trees.

Maude laid still, listening for the outdoor sounds which had turned into proper thunderous noises that kept the baby awake and crying. She was facing the open door, staring at the closed shutters that kept out insects and the great blind moths as big as sparrows who threw themselves out of the dark into the light, their dusty, fluttering wings, their fat bodies hitting the lampshades. The young woman couldn't hear the familiar sound of cicadas, there wasn't the heavy warmth of a coming day. Suddenly, she heard again the sound of thumping feet on the wet ground.

She saw a shadow running towards the house, she had opened a shutter and was leaning out into the dark, listening, looking upwards to the stars that filled the hugeness of the night.

With a lurch of sickness Maude knew.

Mohan was not home yet. Something terrible must have happened.

Baptiste's head appeared by the door, his whole body soaking wet, eyes drawn downwards in great emotion.

'Madame! …. Mohan …' he sobbed, falling on his knees.

'What happened?! … Where is Mohan?'

Maude cried out putting the baby hastily away on the bed. 'Mohan … Madame Oh seigneur! It's terrible, Maude I have lost my dearest friend … my brother' cried the young man in convulsions.

Maude felt the ground throb at her feet. It felt surreal what Baptiste was saying. Mohan, oh No…! God it can't be true …!'

'Baptiste what happened? Please tell me!' implored a broken-hearted Maude. Upon the account of Baptiste of the tragedy which engulfed the St Géran to the tumultuous waters of the bay and reefs, Maude felt the earth shattering under her feet.

Her life came crashing down with an internal implosion worse than the storm, which had lashed on her poor husband.

The baby started crying as if it knew that the worst tragedy that could have befallen upon its frail life had just shattered the silence of the early morning dawn.

Maude looked at the baby in anguish. She lost any understanding of reality and was searching for words to comfort the small bundle of life she cradled closely. She knew they couldn't go anywhere without being persecuted. She had chosen to inhabit a different world in which she grew up. This was finally, that another world. Up to now she had only played on its outskirts, pretending she knew it, but this was the real thing. This was the camp. You couldn't live on a plantation, in a plantation owner's household, without occasionally hearing that word and grasping, however vaguely, that the camp was the homes of the coolies. The downtrodden ones.

The words would be dropped casually into conversation when her Papa had visitors, maybe one of the managers, or a planter from one of the neighbouring estates, and they would discuss in grim tones the Labourer Problem. Somewhere at the back of her mind I had picked up the knowledge that the coolies lived in a camp but had no idea where this was or what it looked like. Until, she eloped with Mohan. Now, this was her world.

During her time living as Grand Missier's daughter, she hardly took note of the coolies themselves. The coolies were part of the landscape. They belonged, quite simply, to the backdrop of life in this grand kingdom of Sugar. Riding out along the back dam, or even from our bedroom windows, they saw them: half-naked men, their skin dark brown and shiny with sweat, their muscles rippling as they hacked at the cane with their cutlasses or bound the cane into bundles and carried them to the canals and loaded the punts. Coolie women, fully clothed, up to their waists in water, pulled the loaded punts along the canals. Coolies were everywhere, so ubiquitous one never even noticed them, and with the wisdom of hindsight she was ashamed to make these confessions. As a teenager, she thought it romantic: coolies at work in the fields, coolies in the trenches. An essential part of the scenery she loved so much, to be taken for granted.

The French colonisers attuned their lives to the weather, to seasonal change, and to the annual cycle of birth, growth, maturity, and death. Yet in the subtropics on Île de France, they found a year-round

195

growing season, year-round summer, and year-round heat with oppressive humidity. They were used to a moderate climate: moderately warm, moderately cold, moderately rainy, moderately sunny. Under the tropic of Capricorn, on this distant island, they had to adjust their eyes to brilliant sunlight, and a palette of splashing colours: vegetation startlingly green, fruits and flowers in flaming reds and yellows, the mountains in shimmering blues and greens, shading to deep purple, the moon and stars radiant and sparkling at night, and the encircling sea a spectrum of jewelled colours from cobalt to silver. They found the Indian Ocean island atmosphere to be volatile: blazing heat suddenly relieved by refreshing showers, and soft, cooling, caressing breezes capriciously dissolving into wild and terrifying cyclones.

'Promised Land' plantation had been now in the De la Tour's family's possession for two generations, had been competently managed by a series of estate managers and slave overseers. Papa Claude, with no prospects of his own in Loire, came here as a young man, temporarily leaving behind his wife and baby daughter. Maman Madeleine and two-year-old Maude followed, once Papa had established himself as one of the legendary sugar patrons who ruled the colony. He built a grand villa worthy of his status. It was constructed of sturdy greenheart mango and tambalacoque woods in the French Colonial style, typical of the land. Sparkling white in the sunlight, with filigree fretwork and latticed lambrequins that provided its ventilation with a full roof of bardeaux tiles. Maude loved the staircases leading to the open terrace, the breeze-filled verandas, the rafters attached to a huge tamarind tree to swing on, the balustrades to balance on.

Most of all she loved the garden: the orchard that brought forth fruits of every imaginable variety, every month a different and more delicious kind; the mango trees with their low-slung branches, inviting to climb. Birdsong and flowers framed their perfect kingdom: the call of the bulbul, the huge bunches of purple, pink and vermillion blooms hanging low from the towering bougainvillaea that climbed the porticos and porches, not to mention the hibiscus, and frangipanis, and oleander, and the rose-fragrance that wafted through it all, carried on the wings of a cool sea-breeze.

They had the vast sky with its puffy clouds, the ocean and the breeze-brushed emerald cane.

Her sister Isabelle and herself ran free and laughed throughout their paradise. They turned from little girls into adolescents, barefoot princesses only vaguely aware that one day they must grow up to marry one of their kind. Maman ran her life based on endless drinks under the veranda with some of her friends. Papa, of course, busy as he was with the estate business, had no time to offer the girls more than affectionate pats on the head and expensive gifts from the metropole.

Isabelle found comfort in Nanny's arms. Behind the laughter, the fun and freedom of estate life, unseen by all, Maude nurtured a great big hole in her heart pining for affection. Until, she met Mohan.

''What I want for each of you,' Papa Claude had said as she arrived from Brittany on that hot Summer day, leaving the grey and gloom of the Atlantic ocean, 'is a sensible marriage with a wealthy young man who can offer you a continuation of the security and comfort you have found in our Île de France.

There are a few such young men in the colony, and when the time comes, I shall certainly ensure that you are introduced to them.'

This sealed her destiny as projected by the patron's status on the island.

Maude had not replied to her father, she knew that he would neither approve of nor understand her.

Chapter 11

Slave

The sea and lagoons surrounding Zanzibar island have always been a magnet to seafarers, who stopped by to enjoy the lush green environment to take a rest from long voyages.

The island bathing in the Indian Ocean awash with stunning fine sand beaches, offered turquoise clear waters where fish were abundant and bigger sea mammals brought their younger ones to rear in the warm shallow waters of the lagoon.

The climate lent to the spices growing freely and soon travellers who discovered them, started trading them, making considerable wealth.

Yet alongside side also came a demand for slaves. Men were captured and chained, to be sent to ships which took them to the various shores where they spent their lives working in harsh conditions under slavery.

Mbawa lived with his parents and two other siblings in a grass and mud hut along the coast from Stone Town, Zanzibar. His father looked after his small plot of land where he grew vegetables, corn, sugar cane, papaya and sweet potatoes. The excesses were sold, by his wife, in the local market, while he fished for dorado, snapper, mackerel and parrot fish. His catch was good, most times and he brought home crab, which he also caught in his nets, for adding to the cooking pot.

Life was inconsequential, the boys growing up with happiness. One day an Omani, one of the latest settlers on the island, came hailing in front of their house.

Mbawa and his mother come out to see who he was and what he wanted.

« Where is your man? » asked Zaffar, the Omani.

« He is not here, what do want? » Mbeki replied, not trusting the look of him.

Mbawa hid behind his mother, peeking every now and then at this goatee bearded man in a long white djellaba, held by a velvet belt, where a dagger was tucked in. The knife was most elaborately carved and studded with sparkling stones.

Mbawa couldn't take his eyes off it.

« I have work to offer and looking for healthy strong men » Zaffar said looking at the woman who had dark shiny skin, in sharp contrast to the bright bold colours of the kitenge she had wrapped around her upper body.

It was in bright patterns and colours and she had metal and beaded jewellery around her ankles.

Surely one of the Masai women who married a local Zanzibari Bantu man. They are known to be tough and very vigilant of their close ones. Zaffar had better be cautious.

The next day, when Mbawa accompanied his mother to the local market to sell some corn,and cassava, they met with Old Kaki who was a regular with her seasonal fruit stall.

Both women shared their daily happenings and Mbawa always valued the wise advice she received from Kaki.

« Yesterday, an Omani came to our house, looking for Mbawa's father, he said he has got work for him. »

« Really? These Omanis are not to be trusted. They take people and their families, never to see them again. No money, no news and when they go to ask, they just get pushed out. »

« You say that! Fortunately, Mbawa's father wasn't at home. » the woman felt relieved, inside, that her husband didn't fall prey to the Omani. « Corrupt men they are, they come and live on our land, and still take our men. »

The Omanis, of many first travellers to Zanzibar, made a series of long--distance dhow journeys throughout the Gulf and down the coast of East Africa. They sailed on favourable monsoon winds to trade mangrove poles, which were used in construction, and foodstuff such as raisins, corn, cloves and dried fish. Cargo was shipped between Muscat and Mogadishu, Mombasa and Zanzibar. The huge demand for strong men to carry out the hard work in the harsh deserts made them trade for humans too. They made most profit from extensive wild -mangrove wood trading, promising locals of wealth they had never dreamed of in their lives. They bought big cows for their meat, and fish and meat would both be dried so they could eat them in stages. For dinner they also ate fish and lentil beans with coconut, and they brought a lot of drinkable water for the journeys from Zanzibar to their land.

Business was booming for the Omanis who had started erecting huge mansions in Stone Town, using the skilled Indians to carve beautiful doors, as a sign of their status. The natural port which existed in Unguja Ukuu was one of the places where the Abbasids, the dynasty who transferred the capital of the -Islamic Caliphate from Damascus to the circular Madinat Al Salam in Baghdad, obtained the slaves that were used to drain and farm the marshes of southern Iraq. It's also during this period that large numbers of African slaves were imported from East Africa into Oman.

A rapid growth of dhows built by the able Keralites for centuries came to Beypore, in Kerala, India for their dhows. This was because of the good timber in the Kerala forests, the availability of good coir rope, and the skilled carpenters who specialized in ship building.

In former times, the sheathing planks of a dhow's hull were held together by coconut rope. Beypore dhows are known as 'Uru' in Malayalam, the local language of Kerala. Settlers from Yemen, known as 'Baramis', are still active in making urus in Kerala.

Zaffar needed more strong men to carry the goods from inland to the ports to be loaded and unloaded to their destinations. The locals couldn't understand distance, in terms of boat voyages on the heavy dhows and the prime wind direction to throw them to the Gulf safely. He went desperately, looking door to door, for more manual workers as demand grew. Not a man escaped his clutches. His master, a powerful man with unknown but impressive great wealth, ruled his workers and slaves with a ruthless brutality. The women in his house, kept behind barred windows and doors, were barely seen with their faces uncovered. He asked for more slaves daily, and Zaffar had to work harder finding them.

As the lucrative trade in slaves and ivory thrived, along with an expanding plantation economy centring on cloves, his master grew greedier.

With an excellent harbour and no shortage of fresh water, Stone Town became one of the largest and wealthiest cities in East Africa. With the coming of Omani rule, there occurred a forced land redistribution as all of the most fertile land was handed over to Omani self-proclaimed aristocrats, who enslaved the African farmers who worked the land.

Every year, hundreds of dhows sailed across the Indian Ocean from Arabia, Persia and India with the monsoon winds blowing in from the northeast, bringing iron, cloth, sugar and dates. When the monsoon winds shifted to the southwest in March or April, the traders would leave, with their ships packed full of tortoise shells, copal, cloves, coir, coconuts, rice, ivory and slaves.

Zaffar started hunting down the chieftains of the small ethnic tribes and dealt directly with them. In exchange for slaves, they got goods from Oman, tobacco and daggers. The latter were objects of great pride and displayed along with the tribal Gris Gris for shows of power and belief of protection. Some of the Bantu men were very strong and chaining them was difficult. Starvation and lack of water in the scorching sun were the only ways to weaken them. Zaffar felt happy when he could bring a hundred of them to his master as he was well rewarded for his efforts.

Every year, about 40-50, 000 slaves from the rest of the regions around the lakes of Tanganyika, were taken to Zanzibar. About a third went to work on clove and coconut plantations of Zanzibar and Pemba while the rest were exported to Persia, Arabia, the Ottoman Empire and Egypt.

Mbawa came to greet his father with a hand of ripe bananas his mother had cut earlier.

Asking for fresh water to drink, the man with glistening skin, loaded in sweat and white patches on his clothes showing the salty crystals; made a quick turn to grab the hand of bananas from his son.

Mbawa loved this moment when his father came back from fishing, he always looked happy to see them and would give a flashing smile.

His wife got some Ugali, beans, and some cassava greens ready to serve to her husband in the hut.

It felt cooler than outside with the sweltering heat.

"An Omani man came to look for you today. He was offering work."

"Work? What sort of work? That would be good to get some extra money. The fishing is getting harder by the day."

"I told him you were not at home; besides he didn't look very trustworthy to me."

Mama Kaki told me that lately men were disappearing, the Omanis have been taking men for work, and their families never hear from them again. When they ask for news from them, they are just chased away"

"Hmm … you shouldn't listen too much to Mama Kaki, she is getting old now. Men go far to work, and maybe there is no way to reply to each of their families."

"But their families never see them again, no news, and no money. Do you find this right? This is indeed strange and alarming. If that Omani comes back, I shall chase him away" Mbeki sounded quite ready to give in to a fight. What would unfurl in the coming days would turn her life upside down.

Zanzibar got its name from the Persians who called it Zangi-bar, the land of black people. Bantus migrated to the country some 3-4,000 years ago, their black skin colour would play to them being preyed upon, to become slaves.

MBeki's husband presented as a potential slave material as per his stature, strength and look. Zaffar did not forget the house, where he missed meeting the man he could've enrolled in his search. So, he came back again, after a couple of weeks.

This time, Mbawa's father was at home, busy mending his nets in the courtyard. His wife was making small corn patties to sell at a local shop.

Zaffar opened the gate cautiously, scattering a few hens which flew to seek cover on some low breadfruit trees. The humid air was stifling. A lone colossal baobab gave shade and fruits which Mbeki turned into sweet flaky pastry on the earthen pot.

"Salamah my friend! I see you are at home today. Well, well …am Zaffar al Umaid, and am looking for strong men to employ to work abroad. Would you like that?"

"Salamah, where is this work?"

"Where you can earn lots of money for yourself and your family. Food and lodging are free. You need to travel and be away for a long time."

"I need to know where and how much you will pay"

"That we can discuss once you accept. Then I can see where you will go, perhaps Oman, Somali, Egypt, even a heavenly place called Mauritius"

"Mauritius? Where is that?! Never heard of it."

"It is a small island just like Zanzibar, in fact the same size, with beautiful beaches and nice masters to work for, and you can be sailing next week, you know!"

Zaffar was extolled his bait to his next recruit.

Mbawa came to sit in his father's lap giving a constant stare to the gentlemen in the long white djellaba. He didn't like the way he looked at him and his father. Something sinister in him, but his young mind could not really understand the reason. His father settled him well and carried on with his net mending.

Zaffar understood that this concluded their conversation. Leaving the courtyard with a bitter cold goodbye, he vowed to get this man at all costs now. He has been playing hard to get, and he too can employ hard means to get him on board one of the dhows.

Mbeki came back from the market to find both her son and husband dozing under the baobab tree. Her heart melted seeing them like that, she wished she could earn more money to make their lives a bit more comfortable. Mbawa heard the ruffle in the kitchen which woke him and ran to his mother.

"Go wake your father, lunch will be ready!"

She fried fish, and served them with some ugali, peanuts and leftover greens. The family ate quietly.

It was enough for them on a daily basis, but commodities were getting more expensive, with the Omanis settling on the island.

They bought all the best fruit and vegetables, and not much was left over for the rest of the local population. If it wasn't for their own vegetable patch, her frequent sale at the market where she could barter, buy other goods, running the kitchen would have been very tough.

Mbawa's father was deep in thought, not knowing how to tell his wife that Zaffar, the Omani, had visited them again. She sure would flare up.

Worst, if she knew his inclination to take up a job with him. He was concerned about his family's welfare too and wanted to do better than just fishing for a meagre income. He still had to deal with the prospect that this was a big decision to leave his family for a long time.

"So, what if I took a job with the Omani? I have heard they pay well."

"Are you out of your mind?! Pay well? So far no one has seen any money coming back. How do you think I will fend alone with our son, sick with worries? Not knowing if you are alive or dead. Not even knowing where you are. That's too much of a risk for some more money."

"Fish are getting less by the day. Overfishing to sell to the hotels is not allowing smaller fishermen like me, to have a good catch to earn a living."

Mbeki looked at her husband, which said enough to close the conversation.

The next day, she got ready to go to the market with her boy in tow, while her husband had made an early sail at the crack of dawn. By midday, she came back home, and was a bit surprised not to see him back yet. She got lunch ready and waited for him for another hour. Nothing.

Mbawa was fed and sent to play with the neighbours' children. By four o'clock, her husband was still not back, and she was sick with worry and fear. She went to some of his fellow fishermen to inquire about him, but everyone was surprised by his missing. They all knew what a good fisherman he was as well as an excellent swimmer. Something was really wrong. Mbeki started to cry and sat under a palm tree scrutinising the sea. She didn't know what had happened to her husband.

Thinking he could do with a good catch as early as possible, Mbeki's husband steered his boat towards the north, before the reef, where fish came to feed. Most of the fishermen he knew didn't have a motorboat with such a strong engine. He saw two men come out on the deck, standing and looking at him.

He carried on with his nets, and when he next looked at the boat, the men had disappeared.

Lost in his thoughts, he didn't pay further attention to the boat and carried on throwing his nets.

Suddenly, a bag covered his head, two pairs of strong arms held him tight and he felt a rope going around him.

He was being kidnapped!

Mbeki's husband had just landed In Zaffar's claws. It wasn't for work.

He would be sold as a slave. Like millions after him.

Chapter 12 - Africa

Africa has been woefully misunderstood and misused by the rest of the world.

Humanity simply does not recognize its debt and obligations to Africa. In western imagery, Africa was the 'dark continent'. A synonym perhaps, but also the potent symbol of a persistent inclination to set Africa and its inhabitants apart from the rest of humanity. The double meaning of the phrase is clear. The 'dark continent' does not refer only to the depths of Africa's equatorial forest, to the density of its tropical shadows, to the blackness of African skin, or even to a widespread lack of knowledge concerning the continent. Above all, the phrase tacitly labels Africa as the place where a very particular form of darkness is found – the darkness of humanity.

In this context, Africa is where people do terrible things, not because the aptitude for such behaviour is a characteristic of all humanity, but because Africa is believed to be inherently more barbaric and less civilized than the rest of the world.

Civilization is not a predetermined consequence of human progress, as the Victorians believed, with white Anglo-Saxons leading the way, the rest of the world following in their wake, and the Africans straggling several centuries behind.

On the contrary, civilization is more like a protective skin of enlightened self-interest that all societies develop as they learn to regulate their interactions with the environment, and with other people, to the long-term benefit of all parties.

Once established for a few generations, civilization might seem durable enough to last forever.

However, the skin of enlightened self-interest is very delicate, easily eroded, and the human capacity for unspeakable barbarity lies just beneath its surface. Africa's tragedies diminish everyone, for humanity evolved in Africa, and we hold everything in common – not least our destiny, now that the limits of global exploitation are understood. Slavery being one of the odds that humans crafted, out of greed.

Mbawa endured a long sea voyage on board of one of the slaves' cargo ships sent to the colonies. It would be nothing short of describing this maiden journey on board a large ship to having been pushed straight down to hell. His life, name, identity was robbed forcefully from him and he was sold as a mere commodity, bearing a number rather than a name. The paradise island where he landed as a slave, became his refuge in his long days and nights of hardship and sorrow. This was a noted criminal act against humanity to kidnap humans and sell them as slaves. White inheritors of the wealth of criminal enrichment remain politically unrepentant and financially dominant.

The ancestors of all humanity evolved in Africa. The earliest evidence of their existence has been found in East Africa, at locations scattered north and south of the Equator; the evidence consists of fossil bones, stone tools and, most poignant of all, a trail of footprints preserved in the petrified surface of a mud pan.

Three individuals – two adults and one juvenile – walked across the pan more than 3 million years ago, moving without evident haste away from the volcano which was puffing clouds of fine ash over the landscape behind them.

Their footsteps took them towards the woods and grasslands which are now known as the Serengeti plains. The human ancestors made their living from and among the animals with whom they shared the landscape. They were diminutive figures, neither large nor numerous, who existed nowhere else on Earth for nearly 4 million years.

The modern human species, Homo sapiens, with a large brain and a talent for innovation, evolved from the ancestral stock towards the end of that period.

About 100,000 years ago, groups of modern humans left Africa for the first time and progressively colonized the rest of the world.

Innovative talent carried them into every exploitable niche. They moved across the Sinai Peninsula and were living in the eastern Mediterranean region by 90,000 years ago. They had reached Asia and Australia by 40,000 years ago, and Europe by 30,000 years ago. They had crossed the Bering Straits by 15,000 years ago and had reached the southernmost tip of South America by 12,000 years. The last remaining habitable land mass, New Zealand, was colonized just 700 years ago.

Africa is only the second largest continent, but it contains 22 per cent of the Earth's land surface. The Sahara Desert alone is as large as the continental United States. In fact, the United States, China, India, and New Zealand could all fit within the African coastline, together with Europe from the Atlantic to Moscow and much of South America. But Africa is much less densely populated, with less than one-quarter of the population of the other regions. Indeed, there are more people living in India (with one-tenth the land area) than in all of Africa. Distances within the continent are vast – 7,000 kilometres from the Cape of Good Hope in the south to Cairo in the north, and approximately the same distance again from Dakar in the west to the tip of the Horn of Africa in the east. The Nile is the world's longest river – 6,695 kilometres from source to estuary; both the Zaire and the Niger rivers are more than 4,000 kilometres long and the Zaire alone drains a basin covering 3.7 million square kilometres, which is larger than all of India (3.2. million square kilometres); on the world scale, only the Amazon basin is larger – 7.05 million square kilometres. Size is one thing, but the position a continent occupies on the globe is also vitally important in terms of the ecological potential it offers a human population. Antarctica, for instance, measures 16 million square kilometres and offers nothing in terms of living potential. Africa, on the other hand, straddles the Equator and offers a great deal. It is the oldest and most stable land mass on Earth, and the evolutionary cradle of countless plant and animal species – including humans. Yet, although humanity evolved in Africa and is self-evidently an expression of the continent's exceptional fecundity, the species appears to have been unable to exploit its full potential within the boundaries of the continent. If modern civilization and technological culture are judged to be the epitome of human achievement, then it is unlikely that the material way of life to which most of humanity currently aspires would have developed if those small bands of modern humans had not left Africa 100,000 years ago.

All the accepted markers of civilization occurred first in non-African locales – metallurgy, settled agriculture, written language, the founding of cities. This is not to make a qualitative judgement. Who knows, but for the influence of the out-of-Africa population, a superior alternative to modern civilization and its technological culture might have evolved in Africa. Indeed, the civilized art of living peaceably in small societies without forming states that were evident in Africa, prior to the arrival of external influences is a distinctively African contribution to human history. In any event, civilization, culture and technology are very recent. if not ephemeral expressions of the human condition. Biology is far more relevant. Here too there are differences that must be explained, particularly in terms of human-population growth potential. The imperial rulers of China conducted a census in AD 2 and found that at least 57.6 million people lived in China at the time.

Written records similarly indicate that the population of the Roman Empire in AD 14 was 54 million.

The population of India during the same period cannot have been less than that of the Roman Empire, and probably at least the same number of people inhabited the Americas and Australasia.

Thus, the modern humans who emigrated from Africa around 100,000 years ago, though possibly numbering no more than one hundred when they left, had multiplied into a global population of more than 200 million people by the beginning of the modern era. Such an impressive growth of numbers is quite within the range of human reproductive capacity and it begs the question: if this was the extent to which the out-of-Africa human population had expanded, how big was the population which had remained within the continent?

Africa is the Earth's oldest and most enduring land mass. Ninety-seven per cent of the continent has been in place and stable for more than 300 million years, most of it for more than 550 million years and some for as much as 3,600 million years.

It is a story of accretion that records a large and significant fraction of the history of the Earth.

A fraction of this history merged with that of the youngest island nations of the Indian Ocean i.e. Mauritius and its sister islands.

Chapter 13

Roots

Shimmering ribbons of aquamarine, cobalt, turquoise stared back at Beti's squinting eyes. She couldn't get enough looking at the sprawling beauty of the lagoons in front of her. Where she sat, laid many scattered seeds of the Casuarina trees in the sand. She picked a couple within reach and felt their spiky outer shells. They were notoriously painful when teachers used to make students kneel on them as a form of punishment. Corporal punishment was much in vogue as a sign of a devoted teacher wishing to savour the progress of students. Parents never questioned nor frowned at the bruised knees of their children.

All was for the best. So, they thought.

Beti's eyes followed a fisherman's boat trying to position the rudder fending the crystal-clear waters of the ocean. A thin white line traced its path behind the boat. Bêti thought it would have taken just a few pieces of wood, a sail and some food with water to go back to their land of origin. None of the slaves nor the indentured workers needed to suffer at the hands of their masters. Yet, it was more complicated than that. The ocean looks calm, soothing and welcoming to the shore. Once you navigate it, it shows you it's real might and true colours.

'I am part of the sea' thought Bêti, as she took off her clothes to reveal a bikini, she was wearing underneath. She kept looking at the ocean. It was like a long invisible arm stretched towards her, summoning her to join it. Bêti touched her toes in the gritty part of the beach where the wavelets lapped in lacy white, minute crests. The water felt cool, but she kept advancing until she was waist high in the water. She looked up at the spotless blue sky and felt that both the blues of the ocean and above her would melt into one vastness. She just had to immerse herself to break the barrier. She dunked her head in the tropical lagoon while she could still see her toes touching the sand, it felt so smooth. When water touched her nape, she felt an immense sense of calmness. In one second, her body fused with the elements and she reciprocated by letting herself go, totally.

'I feel no pain. My mind is blank. My body has disappeared. It was as if I was escaping from myself. Free from all. It felt like an embrace from a mother. Soothing, comforting while your soul feels at rest, and safe.'

She swam for a bit then came out to dry herself under the sun. A light breeze gave her a slight frisson, but the hot sun above quickly dissipated the feeling, asserting its might.

Bêti felt at peace, completely. She had forgotten all the running around, archives, findings, stresses and emotions. She needed to reconnect with the sea to find her footing again. Getting in the water was like an act of cleansing and regenerative strobes to her inner self.

She saw a multicoloured silhouette getting closer.

It was an old lady draped in a saree, carrying a basket of pineapples on her head. She was a regular on this beach, she called herself mama Zanana. She sold juicy and sweet Victoria pineapples to tourists and locals.

Approaching Bêti she hailed 'Bonzour Mamzelle, oulé Zanana?'*

Bêti signalled to her with a positive nod, and she came to her, gave a big sigh and sat down on the sand, lowering her basket.

'Ki ouler mo tifi? Zanana entier ou bien la moitié tranchée? … dis-le pima oussi?'*

'Oui, avec disel pima bien fort'*

'Oui, baba, bien fort, ti pima dans mon jardin sa Bêti'*

Upon hearing the customary 'Beti of an elderly person' to a younger girl, Bêti felt a pinch in her heart, thinking of her Mum. How she would have loved to hear her calling this endearing term to her, once

---

* Bonzour Mamzelle, oulé Zanana? – Good morning Miss, want some pineapple?

* Ki ouler mo tifi? Zanana entier ou bien la moitié tranchée? … dis-le pima oussi? – what do you want my dear girl, Whole pineapple or a slice?

* Oui, avec disel pima bien fort – yes with salt and chilli, the very hot one

* Oui, baba, bien fort, ti pima dans mon jardin sa Bêti – yes dear, the chillies are from my garden, they are very hot

again. She paid the lady and chatted a bit while eating the sweet and tangy pineapple morsels with red hot chilli and salt. Mama Zanana asked her what she was doing alone on the beach. To which she had no answer. The sun was drawing its elongated yellow orange rays to announce it was soon retreating. Bêti packed her towel and headed back to the car. While closing the booth, she noticed the red roofed church by the beach and decided to take a look. It always looked deserted and closed but so pretty that it is one of the most snapped spots by tourists. Its bright red roof contrasted so well with the blue sky and turquoise sea behind. Its shutters were closed and some of the houses nearby appeared empty.

Apart from a small grocery store and a café, the tiny village had no shops.

Walking inside the church felt cool, it was dark and quiet, with the musty odour of crumbling prayer books and ancient stone. There wasn't very much of note, just the usual images of Madonna and Child and rows of votive candles in glass holders flickering before the marble altar. When she advanced up the aisle, Bêti noticed a small woman clad in a skirt and blouse, on her knees in the front pew, her face pressed to her clasped hands.

Bêti decided not to intrude and tiptoed to a seat, taking in the peace and quiet. Churches have this calming nature in them. She felt her afternoon was drawing to a good finish. She headed to the heavy door and emerged into the blinding sunshine.

She had come all this way, hoping to find out more about her mother's ancestry: to piece together the family history that was still only partial. Instead, she had found a mystery to which no one seemed to have the key. It was like catching a glimpse of a secret walled garden through a gateway, only to have the door slammed in your face.

The wilderness of stony beauty in the North Eastern part of the island, stuns by the sight of the black pillow lava rocks of the coast. Here, the waves crash unbridled in loud foamy whites sending mists high up in the air. Waves unfurl in their changing hues of blues known to be ocean like, while the North trade winds blow, making dreamy noises.

Life sometimes stops at the village of Poudre D'Or. It's a charming little hamlet, with small holiday cottages and cosy little shops; picture-postcard pretty, on the face of it, untroubled. Nearby you can stroll on a rocky beach with some stragglers braving the midday sun, with a line and the hope of a catch. Tall breadfruit trees unabashedly balance their football sized fruits and white thick glossy green leaves, while a lone elderly man can often be seen dozing off on a chair nodding to the passers-by. The Indian Ocean breezes make themselves felt here on a constant basis. The strange loveliness of coastal places. There's a sense of continuity, of things unchanged for generations. The senior folks, mostly retired, find themselves counting hours in a day sitting under a tree, throwing bits of bread to lal mounias* and sparrows, reliving news at their own pace. At often

---

* lal mounia – red munia or strawberry finch, is a sparrow-sized bird of the family Estrildidae in Mauritius

times, reminiscing how life was better in the past 'lé temps lontan ti coum sa, a zordi zour zeness vive ene lot manière'*

Bêti stops by the only Chinese shop of the village to get a chilled fizzy drink. From here, where will her steps lead her? She sat down in a corner of the boutique which reeked of white rum and sardines. Two men were in great conversation, each with a clear glass of rum. The rest of the boutique was dark, the only light coming from the large open door. Bêti sat on one of the Formicas covered chairs and opened her iPad on the battered tabletop. She scrolled through the text:

"In June 2020, hundreds of protesters gathered around the statue of Edward Colston in Bristol, England. The statue was made of bronze and stood eight feet high on top of a white Portland stone plinth. Colston was a British slaver. He sat on the board of the Royal African Company for twelve years, during

---

* lé temps lontan ti coum sa, a zordi zour zeness vive ene lot manière – in old times, it was like this, nowadays the youth live differently

which time the company transported over 84,000 kidnapped women, men and children from West Africa to the Americas and the Caribbean, of whom it is estimated over 18,000 died, en-route. The protesters did not believe that this man should be venerated. Two men climbed up the statue and tied a rope around its head, and to much cheering and applauding, the figure was pulled down. The crowd then dragged the statue through the streets and dumped it in Bristol Harbour. Over the next few days, the media was full of stories about the tearing down of the Colston statue. It kicked off a fierce debate in Britain about empire and slavery. About history and memory. About accountability and responsibility. Some said that the removal of Colston was 'erasing history'. Prime Minister Boris Johnson was one of these. 'We cannot now try to edit or censor our past,' he declared. 'Statues teach us about our past, with all its faults. To tear them down would be to lie about our history and impoverish the education of generations to come.'

Others, such as the historian and broadcaster David Olusoga, argued differently. 'The toppling of Edward Colston's statue is not an attack on history,' he remarked, 'it is history.' The demonstration in Bristol was part of a wave of global protests that followed the police killing of George Floyd, an unarmed Black man in Minneapolis, Minnesota. Around the world, people marched in the streets, chanting slogans and carrying signs declaring 'Black Lives Matter' and 'No Justice No Peace'. Strikingly, those taking part were not only Black and Brown, but also White. It felt to many that we were at a moment of profound historic reckoning. The pulling down of Colston's statue and the global protests triggered something in me. An urge to find out more about Britain's role in slavery.

Recently, while researching the book Legacy, I had learned that my mother's family had made money from the slave system. In the nineteenth century, they had sold tobacco from plantations worked by enslaved people of African descent. They were not themselves slaveholders, but like millions of others –

bankers, insurance brokers, sugar dealers, shipbuilders, cotton mill workers – they were part of a broader economy that profited from slavery. I began to feel increasingly uncomfortable about the choices made by my ancestors.

Over the past eight years, the shoe had been firmly on the other foot. I had been working in Germany to restore a lake house that the Nazis had stolen from my father's Jewish family, who had fled Berlin in 1936. Some had found refuge in England, but others were killed during the Holocaust. I had received money from the German government as a token of restitution. It was not only an official admission of guilt; it was something material. This was part of the process of reconciliation. So, if I was willing to identify as a victim in my father's family, to receive reparations from the German government, then surely, I had better understand Britain's role in slavery.

As a child, I was taught that Britain had been the first nation to abolish slavery, that the effort had been led by the politician William Wilberforce, that we were the 'good guys', the great emancipators. I began reading articles and books and was quickly shocked at how little I knew. That it had been British captains commanding British boats operated by British sailors who had transported around 2.8 million captive Africans to the British Caribbean. That it was British families who owned plantations in the Caribbean run by British managers and overseers where hundreds of thousands of enslaved men, women and children were forced to work and die. That it had been British businesses that had transported the cotton, tobacco, sugar and other crops cultivated by the enslaved people to the consumers back in Britain.

How is it possible that common people didn't know any of this?

It was like national amnesia. If Whites of the island people spoke about slavery, which was rare, it was about the plantations. There was barely any mention nor pride shown as to how their ancestors, whose inheritance they are still holding on to, never refer to how they treated a human slave or indentured worker as a commodity. Instead, there are derogatory comments upon the ruling class of Indians.

Bêti realised how depressing it was to delve into the history which had nothing rosy nor heaven like, and the current political landscape was one which has been promulgating cultural and ethnic havoc on a young nation devoid of any identity it can call its own. Finding a plausible explanation as to why a white woman was sharing a tomb with a coolie in a cemetery outside the capital, was one whole huge anomaly which bears no reason.

Mauritius was very familiar with an ambiguous category of labour performed by slaves being "hired out as agricultural labourers."

Then, the racial and socioeconomic logic of the sugar estate were undoubtedly preserved in the transition from slavery to indentured labour.

An often-cited example in this debate is the "double-cut" system, consisting in depriving the labourer of two days' pay for each day off work, whatever the reason justifying the absence.

This double-cut system symbolized the fundamental difference between a slave and an indentured labourer who received a salary. At the same time, this system put in evidence the complexities of indentured labour. Indeed, in a context of epidemics and working hazards, this double-cut system meant that many labourers did not get any salary at the end of the month.

Despite the relevance of comparing the indenture system and slavery, it is obvious that the national construction processes, both historical and contemporary, radically diverge depending on the point of view adopted.

Is it possible to compare the two systems and the fate of the individuals and communities involved?

Is it possible to radically differentiate them, drawing a dividing line in Mauritian historiography between slavery times and indentured labour periods?

There are several Indo-Mauritian identities-finding myths. One of these myths is based on the association of indentured labour with slavery.

There are many tangible hints of this vision of the past in Mauritian politics, making it uneasy to evoke the slave past without automatically including the indentured labour perspective.

Bêti closed down her iPad and left the boutique hailing au revoir, and quickly got into her car. She kept on thinking about how much she learnt about indentured servitude and slavery in school. Hardly anything. With the whole population, apart from the tiny percentage of Blanc, the island was built by those who came chained and bound by unpaid contracts.

Yet, no one has ever made any effort to allow more to flow into the curriculum in schools. The Blanc still are the most powerful and richest, and their lobby to each ruling political party to work in their favour, is fiercely guarded. No one dares to point a finger to any Blanc. Instead, they are the benchmark to developers and 'how things should be done'.

An apology for hundreds of years of abuse and chaining, whipping humans was seemingly far from possible. Why?

After all, the vast majority of those who transported the captured Africans to the Caribbean and the Indian Ocean were White. Similarly, the vast majority of those who 'purchased' these enslaved men, women and children and made them work on the appalling sugar, cotton and coffee plantations were White. The same is true of the shipowners and sailors, bankers, insurance officers, traders, dockworkers, shopkeepers and countless others, including my family, who were employed transporting, processing and selling the commodities back in Britain and France.

As to the general population who gained from the enormous wealth that poured into these countries on the back of slavery, again the vast majority were White. Of course, there were some Black and mixed-race people who helped capture the African men and women who became enslaved by the British. Indeed, the presidents of Benin and Ghana have both acknowledged and apologised for their ancestors' culpability in the slave trade. There were also some Black and mixed-race sailors, traders, plantation owners, even slave owners. Yet, this was on a small scale compared to the systematic brutality of the White-supervised slave societies. No apology.

There has never been 'guilt' in the sense of acknowledging any wrongdoing, an obligation to redress an offence, or understanding of something owed. This is the White Debt. A cultural debt, acknowledging and apologising for the horror that was British and French slavery. A financial debt, compensating for the economic losses endured by the men, women and children enslaved and the generations of their descendants.

'This is wrong! ... so wrong!' Muttered Bêti aloud, clutching the steering wheel. There she was, amidst lost and wiped out records of her own family, showing how unequal a man considered another human because of his class.

Under this vast blue sky, a seeming paradise island, sleeps a nation shrouded in deep prejudice. Segregation and racism didn't grow as rampant as in

South Africa but lay quieter and may work in more subtle ways. Unlike the Caribbean slavery and indentured workers' visibility, that of the smaller islands of the Indian Ocean remain lost in history. The story of everyday industrialised cruelty and damaging legacies still devastate the lives of the descendants of enslaved Africans, despite the ending of slavery almost two hundred years ago. It is the story of a group of people, almost entirely White, who benefited from this system of slavery and whose wealth, both economic and cultural, continues to be enjoyed today. Unchallenged, they remain the predators which benefited from the weaker ones, in broad daylight, without a flinch.

Bêti passed along the old roads, down the sugar estate of Poudre d'Or. She could run her imagination wild and visualise how it was then, from accounts she read. Away from the coast, stood half a dozen slave houses; within each, five or more families slept. About 100 feet long and 20 feet wide, these huts were built of brick made of baked mud, thatched with cane grass and had dirt floors. Indians and Africans mastered the mud and cow dung lépann*. There were no windows or furniture.

Outside the entrance of each structure were the fire pits, where frugal meals were prepared.

A few steps away, behind some rough fencing, were the latrines.

Next, continuing south, came the windmill. This is where the sugar canes were crushed, and the juice piped to the boiling house next door. Here the syrup was clarified, crystallised and poured into the barrels that were delivered each week.

Beyond the farm buildings and the workers' houses lay many acres of cane fields stretching away from the coast. Criss-crossing this land were a series of canals.

On these, floated shallow-bottomed punts, which were used to transport the felled sugar canes to the windmill. Along the edges of the fields ran deep

____

* lépann – mud and cow dung wall washing

ditches, draining the water away from the fields to the ocean. Rainwater ran into these canals which irrigated the fields. In many places, boreholes and springs were used at stations for refilling water for domestic use. The rules on the estate were as simple as they were clear. Do what you are told and do not talk back. Turn up for work on time and work hard.

Do not gather with others before sunrise or after sunset. Do not leave the estate without permission.

Failure to stick to these rules was met with severe punishment. For minor violations, offenders were placed in the stocks, their ankles held between two wooden boards, and deprived of food and water for a day or more. For greater misdemeanours, they were lashed. Some of the overseers and drivers used the whip - a short leather instrument that was sometimes doubled up to increase the force of the blow. Others used a 'bâton l'alouesse' a tall stalk of an aloe plant which split into several long rope-like fibres and was meant to inflict deep wounds. It sliced the skin open, upon impact.

According to the colony's law, an overseer or driver was not allowed to give more than thirty-nine lashes and a doctor was meant to be at hand, in case of need. In practice, these guidelines were rarely followed. The indentured workers were rarely whipped. They had great fear in them and were used to being subservient by the nature of their social status and caste in their villages of origin. They rarely spoke out defiantly to their sirdars and soon became the prized possessions of the sugar estates. The African slaves on the other hand, managed their freedom after the abolition of slavery, although many remained as servants to the estate and the private domains.

Beti's search for answers shifted from potholed roads and sugarcane fields across the North and centre of the island to archives in Port Louis. What she found there, was a revelation. She once thought that her great-great-grandmother must have been an exception. As it turns out, mystery darkened the lives of many women who left India as coolies. The hint of scandal was communal. Some historians have called indenture "a new form of slavery." In many ways, it was; once in the sugar colonies, coolies suffered under a repressive legal system that regularly convicted more than a fifth of them as criminals, subject to prison for mere labour violations, which were often the unjust allegations of exploitative overseers.

The story, however, is more nuanced than that, especially for women. From the beginning, in all the colonies that turned to indenture to rescue their plantations from ruin after slaves were freed, men greatly outnumbered women. This gave women some sexual leverage. They could take new partners, and frequently, they did. Theirs was often a tale of leaving their country, then leaving their men. Even before leaving their country, many had left their men. In some ways, it was a disguised emancipation on a feminist track. Not far from the millennia of culture they came from where matriarchal harmony existed and the Mother cult had been prominent. With the Muslim Mughal invaders came the curbing of women's rights and status in society to reflect the Islamic idealism of patriarchy and male chauvinism. Manipuri, the district where British recruiters encountered women in purdah hiding behind doors, had a reputation as a good place to find women for the colonies. The number of its recruits was so high that one recruiter wondered strangely, in his diary, if it had "anything to do with the existence of canals, and the (as frequently asserted) impotence of men in canal districts?" Women seemed to outnumber men dramatically in the streets. Manipuri was on the road to Vrindavan, in India, the site of a major temple to Lord Krishna, born in the town nearby, according to lore.

In Hindu scriptures, Vrindavan was the scene of Krishna's mischievous childhood exploits. It was there, in ancient forests where peacocks strutted, that he cavorted with the cowherd maidens known as gopis (shepherds), multiplying himself in order to dance and play with each of them. Chief among the gopis was Radha, the consort worshipped as a deity in her own right, but Krishna had multiple lovers, each of them, often, someone else's wife. The faithful read the gopis' ecstatic and erotic love for Krishna as an allegory for the soul's longing for God, a pining sweet with the anguish of the unattainable.

In the sixteenth century, the Bengali saint Chaitanya inspired a branch of Hinduism that departed drastically from those dominant at the time, namely Brahmins.

It contended that the soul would be released from the endless cycle of birth and death through a Gopi-like devotion to the divine, rather than only dutiful conduct, or knowledge in Sanskrit, of the religious texts. This doctrine created much broader spiritual access. It also made Brahmins less important as middlemen to the gods.

Chaitanya believed that birth and bloodlines should not determine caste; instead, devotion should. The sect he developed is known as Vaishnavism, after the god Vishnu, who is its centre of worship and who, Hindus believe, took human form as the carousing lord Krishna. In the early sixteenth century, Chaitanya dispatched his disciples to Vrindavan to make it the sect's base, by laying down physical and theological foundations in temples and texts.

By the time of indenture, Vaishnavism was the predominant form of Hinduism in the areas where most coolies were recruited, especially among the peasants who were its main recruits. By the nineteenth century, Vrindavan had developed a reputation as a shelter for fallen women, where, it was also widely believed, an infrastructure existed for those women to fall even further. Widows and outcast women flocked to the temples and ashrams there.

Chaitanya's inclusive brand of Hinduism made room for them and gave them hope. The hope that with a depth of emotion in their bhajans and chants, their souls too could transcend. Yet, Vaishnavism also carved out a special and unsettling role for women in its more heterodox offshoots, such as the Sahajiya movement. Too much controversy, even within its own ranks, this movement maintained that ritual sex outside of marriage, a kind of extramarital yoga, was the way to spiritual union with Krishna for a disciplined elite. These select few, could either seduce the wives of other men, or they could turn to the only unattached women there were, the very same ones targeted by coolie recruiters.

Widows and outcasts were perhaps as close to gopis as to pilgrims, gurus and ashram managers engaged in this esoteric practice. In many ways, they were ideal.

According to the Tantric-like principles involved, the women chosen as partners had to be special, because the sex itself was supposed to be ethereal, not carnal. They also had to be unmarriageable, because initiates saw unions that could lead to marriage, one of the householder's everyday duties in society, as merely earth-bound love.

To lead to god, they believed, love had to be illicit and elusive; to pursue the divine, pangs were required. Their female partners also had to be discreet, because the men maintained dual identities, keeping up appearances to the outside world, which disapproved, while cultivating an underground, transgressive self. Secrecy was not just desirable or crucial strategically; it became part of the ethos. The degree to which this clandestine sexual ritual amounted to the exploitation of marginalized women, versus a form of religious service by genuine devotees, is murky. This ambiguity continues in Vrindavan, popularly known as the city of widows.

Manipuri's prolific supply of women for indenture, the mystery that led British recruiters to theorize about canal districts and impotence, might be explained by its place on a well-established pilgrim circuit for widows that began in Chaitanya's birthplace in West Bengal, wound its way to Varanasi where their souls could attain their final release, in the ashrams of Vrindavan. It was discovered later that many of the women in Manipuri had begged their way there, en route to the holy site. It's safe to say that the women who found themselves in the town's emigrant depots, suddenly on their way to sugar cane fields at the other end of the globe, were probably not refugees from erectile dysfunction.

Most likely, they had been siphoned from the pilgrims on their way to Vrindavan in search of food, shelter and god.

Widows historically led a precarious existence in India. After their husbands died, they were supposed to negate themselves forever, in a mourning state. For the rest of their lives, they could wear no long tresses, their heads were shaved, no colourful saris, no vermilion in their hair, no rouge on their lips, no kohl decorating their eyes, no bangles tinkling on their wrists. Enshrouded in white, almost erased, they were viewed as inauspicious and shunned by many. They could not remarry, especially if they were upper caste. They could not inherit property. If they had no sons to support them, they were subject to hunger and poverty. And they could be forced to sit on their husbands' funeral pyre, a practice known as sati. In the dozen years before the ritual was banned, in 1829, at least 8,000 widows in Bengal committed sati.

Bêti arrived home exhausted both by the day and her thoughts. She went straight to have a shower, then made a cup of tea. There were not many leftovers in the fridge to heat up for a quick dinner, so she settled

for a piece of baguette with butter and a zinzli*
banana. She settled in front of the TV but soon got
fed up watching the string of ads preceding the daily
seven o'clock Hindi soap operas which turned the
population into zombies. Some dogs in the distance
were barking, showing their territorial defence. Or
maybe they too were just plain bored by their owners
who are by now all glued to their TVs.
Bêti went out and looked up at the starry night.
Shukar* was shining bright and Mars was too. It was
cool tonight, just right, thought Bêti, ready to crash in
her bed. A lizard made itself heard, triggering the
night long cicadas in their conversation.

---

* zinzli – dwarf banana in Mauritius, sweet and plump
variety
* shukar – Venus star

Chapter 14

Rebellion

A year passed after Mohan's demise. Maude was no longer her bubbly self. Baptiste had gone to her parents' house and told Madeleine, the help, about what happened. The latter often sent food through Baptiste and whatever she could sneak out to help her poor young mistress. No one mentioned anything to Maude's parents, fearing for their lives.

One night, Maude ran away like a thief in the night. In the darkness, one hour before dawn, she placed a letter she'd written to Baptiste on the tiny locker by her bed and laid the necklace Mohan gave her upon it. The oil lamp was on in the hut, casting a celestial light upon her child as she slept, oblivious to her treachery. She crept out. Although Maude was running away, it felt as if this was the moment she had stopped running. She could never have gone back to her parents, because then she would have lost her daughter in an even more terrible way. They would have never accepted a coolie's child. She had done the best thing for her family, Maude tried to tell herself. She would now be free from her dark secret. She reached the beach and stood by the shore looking far into the glistening water, lit by the flickering half-moon behind the clouds. Then she walked into the water till she was waist high. She turned and looked behind her, then proceeded ahead this time with the water reaching her shoulders until it went all over her. Immersed, she allowed herself to reach an invisible Mohan under water.

Her body floated back to the shore, washed away just like that of Mohan. Death knew how to bring the lovers together, for eternity.

The fate of slaves and indentured workers resonated with the hardships and humiliation in the same way.

Only their continents were different. Not very much is widely known about the colonial times in the Indian Ocean compared to the West Indies and the Caribbean. In that corner Jamaica stands out in history to have triggered a revolt that would eventually see the abolishment of slavery.

In Mauritius, there were run-away slaves (esclaves marrons) but rarely inflicted great damage or violence to their masters or of their properties.

At that time, Jamaica had long thrived on its image of easy wealth amid tropical breezes, long manor lanes shaded by coconut trees, plenty of fresh mangoes, languid afternoons spent drinking rum-and-lime punch on the veranda while watching one's human property chopping rows of sleek sugarcane. From this vantage point, it was easy to appreciate why this bead of volcanic rock in the midst of a turquoise sea had been singled out by Christopher Columbus as the most beautiful of the islands he had seen in his four voyages to the West Indies. Cooling trade winds buffeted the coasts, the Caribbean looked like a plate of cobalt when spread out for miles against the edges of wide beaches. The island's soils proved ideal for growing the cash crop that planters called Creole cane, the sharp stalks of grass that concealed sweet fibre in their interiors. Assuming no disruptions from hurricanes or slave mutinies, a man who had been given eighty acres of land and enough capital to buy one hundred enslaved Africans could expect to produce eighty tons of sugar in a year, enough for a comfortable living. With more land and human property, he could become dazzlingly prosperous.

The British had grabbed the island in a dishonourable manner. After Oliver Cromwell had taken control of Parliament in 1653 and overseen the beheading of King Charles I, he laid out a plan for seizing more territory from the Spanish as part of an anti-Catholic crusade.

Cromwell aimed to secure a bigger share of gold by issuing merchant seamen 'letters of marque and reprisal,' which made it legal for them to hijack Spanish galleons and claim the stolen cargo for themselves.

Not coincidentally, this scheme also created a foreign adventure through which to distract from the divisions and potential counter revolutions at home. The aggressive "Western Design" campaign led to a 1654 British invasion of the island of Hispaniola with 8,200 amateur soldiers drawn largely from poor white laborers from the neighbouring sugar island of Barbados.

Nothing went right. Cannons went missing, approximately one thousand troops immediately died from malaria and yellow fever, squadrons got lost in the jungle, and the generals grew contemptuous of their own men; one called them lowlifes and braggarts "so cowardly as not to be made to fight."

Another lamented having to march into the jungle with "common cheats, thieves, cutpurses, and such like lewd persons" who were fit more for prison than military service. After blundering around for three weeks, the generals William Penn and Robert Venables decided to switch islands, and they headed to the more lightly defended island of Jamaica, which took its name from a corruption of the name given by the native Taino people, Xaymaca, "the land of wood and water."

The Spanish had already carved it up into plantations and made slaves of the Taino.

Here the British had better luck, burning down the main settlement of Villa de la Vega and then rebuilding it under the new name Spanish Town. After the restoration of the monarchy with the crowning of Charles II, Jamaica became known as a wild frontier outpost where those who sided with Cromwell and helped murder the king could safely hide out from the authorities.

These first Jamaican sugar boomers wiped out most of the native Taino people through disease and slavery, and built a city, Port Royal, at the tip of a slender thread of land that curved around one of the biggest natural harbours in the world—one that could easily have sheltered the entire British fleet. Port Royal's streets were tight and labyrinthine; they were especially dangerous when a ship full of thirsty sailors disgorged its crew after the six-week journey from Britain or the slaving grounds of Africa. Only slightly less populated than Boston, but far more carnal, Port Royal fed off sugar and piracy to support a knot of tailors, blacksmiths, brothels, bakers, from gambling dens, alehouses, a few churches, and even a small synagogue tucked out of the way to serve a small population of Sephardic Jews who spoke Portuguese and had migrated from Brazil. The former Welsh pirate and privateer, Henry Morgan soon learned he could make far more money planting sugar than he could raiding ships.

On December 27-1831, a watchman standing on top of the courthouse in the Jamaican city of Montego Bay spotted a fire on a hillside south of town. Then another fire appeared close by. Then another. The meaning of this chain of fires was instantly clear to the watchman, Colonel George Lawson, who had been, like the rest of his militia unit, in a state of high alert because of credible evidence that the slave population of the northwest shore of Jamaica was about to rise up in revolt.

Lawson reported the fires to John Roby, the collector of customs at the port, who had almost certainly already seen them.

As the Caribbean night sky gradually turned the colour of copper, Roby wrote an urgent message to the governor of Jamaica underlining two words, a gesture almost never seen in official correspondence: « Sir, I consider it my duty to inform you that there is at this moment a serious fire raging in a south-easterly direction from this town, apparently 8 or 10 miles distant, and it is supposed at Hampton Estate but from the glare I fear it extends to other estates in its vicinity lying more to the southward.

From the late insubordination of the negroes on many estates in the neighbourhood, which has caused the militia to be under arms since Sunday last, it is feared that this fire is not from accidental causes and I beg the favour of your giving his Excellency the governor immediate information thereof. »

He then added a postscript, knowing that one company of a badly trained militia would not be sufficient to prevent the white population from being massacred:

« half past 9 I have just been informed that Kensington pen and Mr. Tullock's settlement has been burned—we have one company of the 22nd regiment in this town. »

Lawson and Roby had no way of knowing if the family had been left alive or not. By ten o'clock, the men had counted at least six fires that seemed to blend into a terrifying orange crown on the hills. By this point, Lawson "feared the east part of the parish would be destroyed by morning." If anything, this was an underestimation. Fires were breaking out all over north-western Jamaica.

One man on a plantation in Cornwall started a letter and kept revising it throughout the night: The work of destruction has commenced.

We now see two fires, evidently in the direction of St. James. Ten o'clock -we have just received intelligence that the fire at Palmyra estate was extinguished, after burning down one trash house. Eleven o'clock at night—The work of destruction is going on. The whole sky, in the southwest is illuminated. From our office we at this moment perceive five distinct fires, one apparently in this parish, the others in St. James's and at no great distance from us. Midnight—One fire is raging with unabated fury. We apprehend it to be the whole of the works and buildings on the York estate in this parish. Nobody who saw them ever forgot the plantation fires.

They would burn and reignite across north-western Jamaica for the better part of two weeks and rain a curtain of ash down on the trees. Various awestruck witnesses described them as "one solid mass of flame," "a vast furnace," the skies "lighted up in all directions," a chain of signalling lamps that seemed the fruits of a biblical judgment.

"The whole country," concluded a minister, "seemed given up to destruction."

More than two hundred blazes were reported in the opening days of the revolt, and in the daytime, they magnified the glare of the tropics and tinted the sun with menace as an organized army of enslaved people held their master's hostage and fought off attacks from the volunteer militia. The gathering inferno frightened George Lawson to the point that he ordered his post abandoned.

"I am convinced the contest must be decided in the streets of Montego Bay," he hurriedly wrote to the governor before he left for the countryside to link up with another regiment. Professional British soldiers sailed into the harbour three days later and quickly became ensnared in a guerrilla war they were ill-prepared to fight. Many of them expressed astonishment at the military talent of the enslaved people, who outnumbered whites on the island by ten to one.

The rebels built a fortress atop Greenwich Hill and won at least one direct head-to-head confrontation on the battlefield. Indicating an unprecedented level of preparation, some of the dead fighters were found wearing uniforms: blue coats with red sashes. The entire plantation society of Jamaica came under attack in the largest revolt it had ever faced.

One of the richest sugar growers in Jamaica, Richard Barrett, watched the fires with mounting fear from a house in Montego Bay. A fierce defender of slavery, he was the cousin of the poet Elizabeth Barrett Browning and well connected in British society. Barrett scratched out a note to the colonial governor on the fourth night of the insurrection: "The militia to a man are zealous and loyal, and no praise can be too high for their courage and conduct." A hint of his panic, however, can be seen in the drops of ink carelessly spilled onto his note.

"It is supposed that a hundred plantations and settlements are already in ashes," Barrett wrote.

"If the rebellion spreads, our force is quite insufficient to put it down, all depends on the moral effect of the employment of the King's troops. Five rebels have been tried by court martial and shot. A woman also condemned was spared, I think she should be hanged."

Those first nights full of fire touched off five weeks of burning, looting, crop destruction, court-martials, on-the-spot executions, severed heads mounted atop poles, and outright human hunting for sport that shook slaveholding Jamaica to its foundations and sent authorities on a manhunt for the renegade Baptist deacon Samuel Sharpe, who had told his followers the revolt would be a peaceful sit-down strike, only to watch it gyrate out of control and erupt into an inferno.

The violence created alarming newspaper headlines across the ocean, forcing Richard Barrett to return to London to answer for the embarrassment in an attempt to save the three-century-old institution of British slavery. He could not; the costs were too high. The violence on the Christmas holiday played a central role in convincing the British public that slavery could no longer be countenanced and spurring them to demand change from a dysfunctional Parliament.

The effects would also ripple in the United States, where politicians with Southern sympathies had just weathered the revolt of Nat Turner in Virginia and seen how Sharpe's rebellion in Jamaica had led directly to British abolition. Periodic slave insurrections were taken as a fact of life in Jamaica, even as a routine cost of doing business.

However, Sharpe's movement was different: resistance on a dazzling scale.

It was well organized, spread across a wide geographic area, and inspired by Baptist salvation thinking.

More than thirty thousand enslaved people were eventually brought into a plot rooted in nonviolent idealism that anticipated twentieth-century movements such as those led by Mahatma Gandhi, Martin Luther King Jr., and the proponents of liberation theology in Latin America.

Chapter 14 - Nainee

Baptiste swallowed a mouthful of sugared rum, which warmed his throat and made his head swim in sweat. But it felt good. After someone reported finding Maude's body beached, he had run with all his might to the site. The white face of an inert lifeless Maude was too hard to look at, he clenched his fists in agony. 'Ti baba! …. ayoo non! Ti baba*' he darted straight to find Maude's baby.

What he saw broke his heart. He fell on his knees and sobbed violently. The baby was peacefully sleeping as if nothing ever happened.

'Tonton Baptiste will look after you, my angel.'

He promised while lifting the baby and cuddling it gently. Hell had broken out over this sweet couple. It

---

* Ti baba! …. ayoo non! Ti baba – the baby … oh no, the baby

seemed that even the heavens did not approve of their union.

Dusk had fallen as Bêti headed back home after spending the day digging in the records at the archives. She skirted the pond next to the house that was now a dark oval, brushed by moonlight, weary in both body and spirit. Shadows gathered under the trees and the sky had darkened from gold to violet to indigo, the stars twinkling so high above like promises, no one could keep. She drew a deep breath, breathing in the island she so loved, the sharp tang of ambarellas and vavangues*, the sun-warmed scent of raat-ki-Rani*, the local jasmine and birds of paradise lilies that lingered on into the evening, the honest, earthy smells of animal and dirt. In the twilit distance, a mournful sound was heard.

* vavangues – Spanish Tamarind found in the Mascarene islands (Mauritius, Reunion, Seychelles, Rodrigues, Comoros)
* raat-ki-Rani – Indian Jasmine

Bêti let her breath out in a disconsolate sigh. She could now piece together the jigsaw but would reluctantly need to accept the picture. She had come to a dead end, and she could not advance any further, for lack of written records. It is right to close the top on this sad episode, on her maternal side of her ancestry. All she could be right about, was the deep connection she felt for her people living in this land. Everyone is somehow connected to each other. Blood, class and caste mingled without anyone alive to give solid evidence as to who is who, for sure.

Bêti sat by the window, letting the cool night air sweep over her. She could smell the damp soil of June and the freshness of the lake water, hear the distant call of the mynahs and she closed her eyes, letting the island's smells and sounds seep into her, imbibing her with strength.

No matter all she had once hoped for, and lost, this was home and always would be.

Memory lives in light, she thinks. Benevolence and redemption, too. Light illuminates all, even the darkened hollows. The sundials' mad circles have slowed, and the time for concealment had run out. Secrets are just wild birds. They cannot be held captive forever. Soon the night will slowly be bleached out when the new sun will emerge from the dark sky.

Dawn brings hope while dusk only melancholy.

Bêti started to write all she had discovered and learnt. It didn't matter if no one read it, but she had to do it.

« I am a reluctant migrant, connected to my home by fragile threads that stretch across continents. They are too frayed now to hoist me back to the life I knew, to the girl I once was. Yet sometimes a longing for the place of my birth takes hold of me, and it pains me to be torn from all that was familiar to me. »

The sun kissed the surface of the blue waters before it began its slow descent into the bay, overstretching Pointe des Lascars. In the quiet old Creole house overlooking the rocky beach, you could almost hear the hiss at the exact moment the sun and water collided. The roar of an engine pierced the waiting quiet like a knife, stirring the stale air into the beginnings of energy. The quality of the stillness in the house changed from melancholia to anticipation. When the car doors opened, little children's voices mingled with their parents'. It seemed a serious change had come.

In the fast fading daylight, the sound of closing car doors echoed through the house, like thunder rolling across an immense empty plain. The floorboards creaked with expectation, and doors stood ajar with attention. The house braced itself for the new occupants. In a room on the upper floor, sat a man with eyes lost in emptiness.

Baptiste waited to hear the voice of Marie Noelle who had brought the children of Maude's sister on her weekly trip to the neighbouring village market. She would often stop by to see Baptiste and little Nainee. Maude and Mohan's daughter now live with Baptiste and his wife with their two daughters. None of the girls knew about Nainee, not being their blood sister. After the disaster struck, Baptiste sent someone to inform Marie Noelle of the grand la case. Maude's mother came to see her daughter's body and wept quietly, turning her head away. It was decided that the body would be cremated as per Maude's wishes in the letter she left for Baptiste. Maude's mother bought a space in Bois Marchant and gave some money to Baptiste to arrange for a tombstone. The young man made sure that both husband and wife were united on the epitaph. Life carried on and Nainee grew up with her siblings but bearing her father's name - Mohan. Nothing was ever mentioned about her mother nor of her family who owned most of the sugar estates, mills, and workers in the North East of the island. Madame De la Tour kept it a secret from her husband that their daughter died and left a baby orphaned.

For him, she had ceased to exist. Written off as a bad account. His pride and status were far too important to him. Keeping power over estates was primordial in this land. Madame De la Tour sometimes came over for a short visit to see Nainee and she would hug her and look at her hazel eyes with her own misty eyes.

Her Maude lived with the little girl and she had to fight hard not to shout out loud to the world. Social class and 'owning' humans had rigged their humanity.

A ridge far too wide between the slaves, indentured workers and them, the Blancs.

The bonds between Baptiste, his wife and children were strengthened by the half-truths told in order to survive in a world which judge women harshly.

He vowed to keep the shocking truth from Nainee, just as her mother would have done.

He accepted, as so many did, that some secrets are kept for a reason; some secrets must never be told. It will be a sad story of loss and hope, of enduring love and the unshakeable bonds that bind generations through all life's pain.

It is one, of secrets and lies and the will to survive. Resilience unbound driven by hope for a tomorrow not predicted to be any better.

When I was born, my father chose to call me Nanee (beautiful eyes). In our Bhojpuri language, Nainee was like the doe eyed gazelle, the most beautiful and graceful animal in the new forests Grand Missié had brought onboard ships from Java. I was my father's first child and he thought I was the prettiest daughter ever.

Our village backed onto a huge rock that towered above all the mud huts below. Behind this rock, the mountains rose above us, high into the sky. In fact, the village was ringed with mountains on all sides. In just fifteen minutes you could walk out of our village and lose yourself in the foothills. Our home consisted of a rectangular compound, enclosing two mud huts facing each other. This we called the camp. The newest part of the camp had long stone-built hangars which sheltered the malbars. Ours was fenced around with a wall of wooden posts, interwoven with straw. Two benches ran down each side, where we would gather around a fire in the evening and laugh and tell stories while mama cooked us dinner. My father always slept by the door to protect us. He wondered if there were snakes and hyenas in the forest and hills nearby and I was afraid that they would come in and grab me. Little did he know that the island was far from the jungles of Africa. It was devoid of any mammals and venomous creepy crawlies. There once were Dodos, which were enormous pigeon-like flightless birds, but they had been entirely decimated by the Dutch and Portuguese who once tried to settle on the island. Devoid of any source of food, they gorged on the poor trustworthy Dodos, which didn't take humans as their predators.

As the eldest child, I helped Ayala, my mother, starting from an early age. By my seventh year, I was fetching wood and water from outside the fence and sweeping the area surrounding our hut. By my twelfth year, I was also entrusted with the care of my two younger brothers and three sisters. With my duties done, Mama would let me play with the other girls and boys of my age. Sometimes, just before nightfall, we children would gather at the centre of the camp's compound and watch the grown-up's light fires to chase away mosquitoes. Even now, I see TiColo coming towards us, leaning on a forked stick. Everyone would stop talking as he sat. He was always aided by the same young man who seemed to await his arrival.

"This evening children," TiColo would say, "I shall tell you a story, you will always remember."

The old man would look at the sacred forest outside our fence and ask the spirits for permission to begin the story. When they gave it to him, we would clap our hands and beg him to start. His stories were sometimes frightening, but they always ended with the good spirits defeating the bad ones. To this day my voice trembles when I tell children the story of Zanfoute, the disobedient girl who was taken away by the bad spirits. One memory that remains with me, was the day Grandma took me on a journey to receive the blessing of our ancestors. The night sky was crowded with stars when she came to wake me. She led me along narrow paths, across several streams, through bushes and past huge baobab trees standing sentinel in the warm night. Even though I was twelve,

I found it difficult to keep up with her pace. Fortunately, she would stop and listen each time we heard a noise. Then she would whisper the name of whatever it was that had made the noise. I held on to her hand and wished the moon would light our way. Just after we had crossed a stream, we heard shouting and wailing. We paused and then, as the noise was coming closer, we hid beneath a bush. Two men stopped in front of our hiding place. My heart was pounding like a drum: Grandma held my hand tighter. We could hear the sound of their urine falling on the leaves where we hid. We stayed as still as chameleons waiting to catch their prey. After the two men had finished, they waited until the people had gone. As the group moved away, Grandma stood up without speaking. Later, she told me that she had counted the silhouettes of twenty men and women yoked together, and other men, with long batons, leading them.

Instead of continuing our journey along the path, Grandma went deeper into the bushes, scaring the insects and sleeping birds. The rays of the rising sun were penetrating the undergrowth when we emerged to find an enormous tree in front of us; its humid leaves gave off a strange smell that lingered in the morning air. Grandma took a dried calabash's shell from her bag, held my hand and walked towards the tree. She poured the contents of the calabash, so they trickled onto a polished white stone next to the tree, saying, "Grands l'esprits nou zancets*, you, who have always protected our people, guide us safely to our destination. We travel not to seek harm for others, but to seek good for ourselves and our loved ones."

We then sat with our backs against the tree. It was not long before a cool breeze made way for the spirits, and multi-coloured leaves drifted in the air as the fragrance of herbs and flowers filled our senses. I watched Grandma's face, knowing that the ancestors had answered her prayers with a perfumed blessing. The sun was still low when we moved on. Whenever we heard people approaching, we hid and continued only when they had passed. Grandma kept away from people and villages; in some places, charred

---

* Grands l'esprits nou zancets – great spirits of our ancestors

sugarcane and bushes remained where lush green fields once stood. Even at a distance, the smell of burnt sweet canes lingered in the air. I was tired, hungry, and thirsty, when, just before the sun was overhead, we reached our destination, a village. It was next to an enormous basalt boulder and had a closed entrance protected by upright trunks. At the barrier, grandma made a clicking sound with her tongue, a sound that was repeated by someone from inside. Men with bulging arms shifted two trunks, allowing us to enter. The camp was full of activity, women pounding cassava for the daily meal, men fashioning hoes, children sweeping and the younger ones chasing chickens, goats, as well as each other. Once the young ones had noticed us, they followed us, and their questions tumbled over each other at such speed that it was impossible to answer them all. Grandma greeted everyone as we made our way to the camp's elder. After exchanging greetings, she presented him with a wooden bowl that Papa had made.

He caressed the bowl with his wrinkled hands and nodded his head in appreciation. He gave permission for us to stay.

Grandma thanked him and then led me to an acacia tree on the edge of the camp. A waft of herbs greeted us as we approached the tree with its gnarled, exposed roots. Had it not been for the movement of a head covered in white hair, I wouldn't have noticed the man sitting on a mat under the spreading branches. His body seemed to merge into the exposed roots. I bowed my head three times as Grandma did.

The man's face was creased like that of a wild boar and his skin hung in folds from his body. His eyes were cloudy, and his front blackened teeth protruded over his lower lip.

Pointing at the mat in front of him, we sat where we were asked to.

After exchanging greetings, Grandma offered him cassava and grains that she took from her bag. Thanking Grandma, he then asked, "Was your journey pleasant?" She replied that the ancestors had protected us. He untied the strings binding some dried leaves, took part of one as well as a pinch of dried herbs and sprinkled both on the small charcoal fire next to his mat.

A plume of perfumed smoke rose up and then spread around us; it made me feel light-headed.

Rubbing his hands together, he asked, "Did you encounter anything unusual on the way?

Life is intolerable here.

It will not get any better but in fact will become much worse. It is urgent that the elders take a decision whether to move our people to where the sun sets."

Looking at me with his clouded eyes, he asked, "What about this little creature?

She needs to be protected?" Grandma nodded.

From a pouch, he took a handful of cowry shells and placed them face down on the mat.

He lifted his face to the sky, closed his eyes and recited words that I didn't understand.

He became silent and his face had a far-away look.

After a while, he lowered his head and, as if with difficulty, opened his eyes. He was like a man who had just woken from a dream. Closing his eyes again, he rearranged the cowries as he chanted, his voice barely audible. His head moved up-and-down when, sightlessly, he pointed his calloused finger at the shells furthest from him, saying, "It's a dangerous time for our people.

The greatest threat comes from the direction of the rising sun."

Opening his eyes, he regained his faraway look. His lips moved as if he was talking to someone. He then picked up a cowry shell and looked at the underside.

"Evil spirits do not only come from far away; they are also among us. Wherever they come from, they have bad intentions. This little creature has nothing to worry about. I am here to protect her."

He opened his other hand and placed it under Grandma's chin. She undid a knot on the side of her kitenge, her wrap around, and removed the carving that my father had made for me and gave it to the wise man. His calloused fingers felt it and found a small hole. He added other herbs and what looked like tiny wood shavings to the small fire. A woody camphor-like smell filled the air, different to anything that I could imagine. As the fire died, he closed his eyes and recited strange words as he stirred the embers, until only ash was left. He put one gnarled finger in the ash and brought it to his mouth. His tongue touched the ash; he nodded, satisfied, and only then, opened his eyes. He took a pinch of the ash and pushed it into the hole, and, with great ceremony, repeated the action three times. With a wooden rod, he pressed down the contents and sealed the hole. He used a hooked knife to remove the protruding part of the rod. No mark or change of colour was apparent when he had finished. Concealing the carved amulet within his cupped hands, he closed his eyes and again recited some strange words. He then took a plaited fibre, passed it through the amulet and hung it around my neck, and said, "Always keep this on you and the ancestors will protect you from evil spirits."

He looked at Grandma, then at me. "Child, your father invoked the ancestors when he made this amulet. In this amulet, the voice of Africa is heard. It is the most powerful amulet that I have touched."

I grasped it warmly in both hands. My little pounding heart was light, and I felt secure, protected by the ancestors and the amulet that Papa had made. The wise man pointed his stick at the Vacoas mats on the other side of the tree and told Grandma that we should rest there until we were ready to go home. Grandma stood and bowed three times. She then made that peculiar sound that she had made when we stood before the entrance of the tree-size trunks. The old man smiled, and we left him. The villagers brought us food and drink before encouraging us to rest.

I was in the deepest sleep when Grandma woke me. The moon was overhead when we started our return journey.

As we made our way up the hill "Grandma," I asked, ''what type of animal is an afree-ca?'' She stopped and turned.

Grandma said that she had never heard the word before, but that it was probably a special word used by wise men. I knew that the wise men were much wiser than anyone else.

My mother would encourage me to play, after I had helped with the daily tasks and some hours in the fields. She would say, "Nainee, go and play. Before you know it, you will be taken away from this and you'll be a woman." Although there was sadness in my mother's voice, I didn't know what it was to become a woman.

So, Mama said it was the start to being good wives and mothers, afterwards in life. Once my monthlies would come, my days of playing and wandering with boys would end, that is, until I found a husband.

One day papa Baptiste called me and asked me to sit down beside him.

'Nainee, I have something to tell you, now that you are able to understand things a bit better.'

I don't know why this sentence frightened me. I felt something was going to happen that would change everything.

I was right.

'Nainee you are my beloved eldest daughter and you know how much papa loves you, but in reality, you are not my real daughter I mean my own blood'

I listened dumbfounded, like in a trance, as if someone had knocked me hard on the head.

'You see, your parents died when you were still a tiny baby. Your father Mohan was my best friend. He drowned at sea while trying to save lives.'

Enough was said, tears came out from nowhere and rolled down my cheeks feeling hot. My vision blurred and the man in front of me no longer looked like my papa.

He suddenly was a voice uttering words which I didn't comprehend but gave me an ache inside.

'Come here, my Nainee' I went to him and accepted his warm gentle cuddle. One I have always loved and felt safe.

'Papa tell me what you are saying is not true.'

'I wish it was, I have broken my own promise. But I need to tell you the truth. You have your family. Your grandmother is still alive.'

'I have another grandmother?!'

'Yes, you do. And this is from your Mother, Maude'

'Maude …Maude' the word felt alien, but I couldn't stop repeating it.

Papa handed me a small necklace made of shells, it had a mother of pearl pendant which caught the light and shone in iridescent colours. His hands trembled while he handed the necklace to me.

Afterwards, he covered his face and sobbed like a child. I had never seen papa cry.

'Papa don't cry, please tell me why you are so sad. I don't want another grandmother if that makes you so sad. I am your Nainee, remember?'

'My child, this breaks my heart to see you living like us each day. You are meant to be like a princess with me and mama working for you.'

'What are you saying? This makes no sense, why would you work for me? Are you trying to punish me? What have I done wrong Papa, what?'

Sobs drowned my words and papa embraced me; we both were crying. He knew why, I didn't. There was surely hurt on both sides. I left the necklace on the bed, next to papa.

'I don't want it. Mama is my real mama.'

'No! You promise me that you will keep it safely. That's all you have of your mother and …. this.' He produced a small black and white photograph with scalloped edges. It was a family gathered around a seemingly very elegant veranda. Like that of Missié Blanc. I looked at it closely, through my blurry eyes. I wiped them with my hand and looked closely.

'See, this is Maude, your mother, and here are your grandparents.'

My small world came crashing down, for good this time. I could see the masters in this photo, and no one who looked like papa, and mama. They were white.

Mama entered the hut and stood surprised to look at the state of us.

'What's going on?' Papa gave her one look. There were no words needed.

'Nainee, it's time to get your godna (tattoo), Nani Champa has come over from the other camp to get it done to you.'

I turned to papa beckoning an acknowledgment, now that I seem to have a different identity.

'Yes Nainee, go and get it done. Your Papa Mohan also had one like his mama too.'

'And mama Maude?'

Papa Baptiste's face clouded, and he bent his head. Mama took my hand and walked out of the hut.

In the other hand, I was clasping the necklace and the photo.

Chapter 15

गोड़ना – Tattoo

Godna or tattoo is an ancient artform practiced by the Gond tribe of Chattisgarh in Central India.

Godna has many motifs, each having a specific significance — some are curative in nature, while others are applied according to rites of passage in a woman's life, such as puberty, marriage and childbirth.

The tattoos are highly valued for their powers of healing and their ritualistic significance. Many people of north India carry tattoos as a mark of identity belonging to a certain group or ethnic community. From being used as a sign of status to jewellery-like markings, tattoos have been around in India since ancient times.

However, just how old this custom is, remains a mystery. From the dense, rain-soaked mountain jungles of the northeast to the dry deserts of the Rann of Kutch in the far west, tattoos have not always been about beautifying the human body; they have been used for diverse reasons by different communities across India. In Southern India, permanent tattoos are called pachakutharathu. They were very common, especially in Tamil Nadu, before 1980. The nomadic Korathi tattoo artists travelled the countryside in search of clients.

The kollam, a sinuous labyrinthine design believed to ensnare evil beings, is inked on bodies to permanently keep them safe and secure until reunited with deceased ancestors in the afterlife. Among the Toda tribe of South India, the hands and calves and shins are tattooed with the same geometric patterns used in their embroidery. Most patterns were inspired by nature. Many also created jewellery-like patterns around the neck, earlobes, arms, wrists, ankles and backs. The simplest pattern was a bindoo (dot). It would appear on the forehead, cheekbones and chins. Writing 'Ram' was considered auspicious as well as having a lotus on the forearm.

Many indentured immigrants had their names tattooed, as well as a swastika, Om, a simple five petal flower or a triangular pattern of dots. Some who hailed from tribes and untouchables had facial tattoos which identified their tribes.

Boys are also decorated with tattoos. The elders explained how tattooing was a very ancient custom, even before white men brought them to this island. Tattooing is even more important now, they would say, because the brown and white men think that the spotted tattoos are signs of smallpox and leave the coolie women alone.

The acacia shrubs were covered with flowers, and the air was filled with a sweet smell and the buzz of bees. In seven sunrises I would be taken away for my initiation, that is, given a turmeric water bath as a cleansing ritual and given a godna.

I was daydreaming close to our hut when I overheard two boys, Tapo and Manon, talking about collecting honey the next day.

"Can I come with you?" I asked.

"No. It's too dangerous for a girl."

"Please, please!"

"It's better for you to stay in the village and wait for the bees to come and sting your chest. Then you'll have beautiful breasts for your initiation."

They laughed, put their arms around each other's necks and swaggered away. I wanted so much to go with them, before my initiation, but from their giggles I knew they didn't take me seriously.

That night, my dream of eating honey was so vivid that I awoke in the middle of the night with my mouth watering. I stayed awake and planned to join the boys on their adventure of collecting honey. Mama woke me early in the morning.

'Nainee! Wake up … we are going to the river. You should come too.'

'No mama it's too early, I am sleepy.'

'Just get up!'

Mama huddled the sleepy head, among other women of the camp, whispering and giggling. One of them gave me a poke with her elbow. 'So, you are now a young woman!' She giggled. I am now very annoyed, and fully awake. Certainly not ready for an immersion in the cool water of the river. Mama encouraged me to do so, and said 'hurry, wash yourself fully and your hair too. Today, Nani Champa will come to see you'

'I don't want Nani Champa to see me … not anyone else, and for what reason?'

'Because you had your first monthly, silly girl!' There goes the giggle again. I remembered the stickiness between my legs and immediately felt shy.

'Alright mama, but please cover me'

My full ablutions done, hair washed, I felt fresh and ready to face the day. Nani Champa came after tea, while mama bid her to sit on a pidha* papa had made.

'Kahan godey ke Beti?*' She said in her native Bhojpuri, which mama and I understood perfectly.

My mama Maude with her light hair, flashed to me.

'Nani, Grand Madame bhi godna Karela?*'

------

* pidhat – small low stool used in India
* Kahan godey ke Beti? – where do you want to have your tattoo my gilr?
* Nani, Grand Madame bhi godna Karela? – GrandMa where does the great Lady have her tattoo done?

Nani stared at me and pulled her sari to cover her head while her jhumki* showed its star shape studded with white stones.

'Eh baba, ka bola thawe ge! Madame godna kahan karba, utta blanc hawe na.' 'Oh dear, what are you saying? Madame doesn't do godna, she is a white, isn't that right?'

'I am also not doing any godna then, because my mo….!'

Mama lunged forward and shut my mouth, covering it with her hand. Nani stopped and looked at us. Mama said 'Nani, would you like some cha? Nainee come and help me for a minute, will you?'

I followed mama to the kitchen.

'Nainee you are never to utter what papa told you! Do you hear? Never, means never. Or both me and your papa will be dead.'

'But mama ….'

'No, I don't want you to ever repeat those words.'

---

* jhumki – dangling inverted cup shaped Indian earings

'Mama I don't want to have a godna. My mama Maude …didn't have one.'

'Shhh …she said. Not a word. If you don't want a godna fine, I will tell Nani that we don't want to have one done now.'

A confused me was happy enough to face Nani and leave to do other chores. I wasn't having any godna done! It was my first step to connecting with my mama Maude.

Chapter 16 - Gros Noir

In May 1873, the price of slaves was high on the East African coast, and the dealers on the Zanzibar waterfront made no secret of the good season they were having. Slaves were coming into the island in large numbers that year, conveyed from the mainland in small, shallow-draft open-decked sailing dhows of the Swahili coast.

Most of them came from the little town of Kilwa, 170 miles to the south of Zanzibar on the mainland of Tanzania, since that was where the main route from the great slave-hunting grounds of the interior finally reached the sea.

The journey north usually took two days, and the slaves, packed in tight rows, were given water, but little else, and often arrived in a desperate condition. The long march to the coast had taken months and had left its mark. Afterwards, cooped in barracoons in the marshy, malarial country at Kilwa, many became sick, and when they were delivered at the Zanzibar waterfront, they were emaciated, and often traumatized by the long ordeal. Wrenched from their homes, physically abused, sold and bought many times, they had little sense of where they were or what was expected of them. They had witnessed and experienced terrible violence. The women, deprived of their children, were constantly raped on the trail. The men, often summarily beaten, had seen many of their companions mutilated and killed. The higher born Arabs of Zanzibar considered them to be barbarians, pagan Africans who spoke no Arabic or Swahili, and regarded them with aversion and contempt. Thought of as little more than beasts, sometimes branded like animals, they were disembarked at the Customs House, a collection of shacks and yards above the quay, which extended out into the stinking mud.

Gros Noir, his new name as a slave. The 'owners' never bothered to keep his African one, slaves were given haphazard names based on how they looked and what fancied the owner. Gros Noir here means a big guy instead of grand since this would mean a higher status, like Grand Missier, which only the Colonial master could be called. He remembers how many days and nights he stood chained waiting for his fate. Shock and disbelief of having been trapped and captured like an animal, had given way to plain passivity. His inner ache of being snatched from his family, bore a hole in his soul.

How could humans inflict such a wound to a fellow human?

In the night, the women would be casually abused, the men beaten by other slaves, specially employed to 'season' the latest purchases i.e. men who perhaps themselves had been through this very process, years before. Finally, when the new captives were ready, they too were brought to market, and the best ones sold for a handsome profit. These early months of the year were a time of great activity in Zanzibar. The harbour was packed with triple-sailed, Arab dhows that came down from the Persian Gulf with the north-east monsoon every year to trade goods before returning with the changed winds. They brought dates, salt fish and ghee, and they returned with ivory and hides, beeswax, some gold dust and slaves – just another commodity, but one which was increasingly valuable in the countries of the north. For during the last two seasons, along the Somali coast of Africa, on the Red Sea and in the Gulf ports of Persia and Arabia, demand had been unusually high.

Between 1869 and 1870, a cholera epidemic had scythed through the cities and towns of the Middle East, and the slave populations of the region had been reduced, by up to half. As the households and factories, the palm estates, fisheries and stonework of the area attempted to rebuild their workforce, prices had soared. Zanzibar, one of the last major sources of slaves in the world, was having a good year.

That season, over 20,000 slaves were exported from the island, and most of them went north and across eastbound to Madagascar to pick more slaves and head to Mauritius.

The British authorities in India, who had responsibility for policy over the Indian Ocean, knew, but the slave trade was of no interest to them. In London, the politicians professed to be concerned, but did little beyond paying for the few warships necessary to keep public opinion happy. Most of all, the acting consul in Zanzibar knew, for he, more than anyone, had studied where the dhows went each year and how many slaves they carried. There was a kind of conspiracy to allow this secret trade to go on, to pretend it was under control, because it was in everyone's interest to do so, and to leave the status quo undisturbed. Nevertheless, because under law, the trading of slaves was forbidden throughout the British Empire, in 1867 a Vice Admiralty court had been set up by treaty in Zanzibar to adjudicate over dhows caught smuggling slaves. In some ways, having ship loads of indentured workers from Calcutta was considered legitimate and brought no administrative troubles.

For over three hundred years, Europeans had used slave labour from Africa to develop their colonies in North and South America and the Caribbean. Britain, during that time had become the greatest beneficiary and the most extensive practitioner of the traffic. However, it was also the British who first developed an intense moral repugnance against what they most of all, had encouraged and practised.

Although few were aware of its scale, in the Indian Ocean a trade not dissimilar to the Atlantic traffic, went on virtually unimpeded. Throughout the nineteenth century, tens of thousands of Africans continued to be taken each year and exported via the Red Sea and the ports of the Persian Gulf into Muslim Asia. It was even suggested that the East India Company was complicit in allowing this business to survive and prosper.

Among those who knew 'the East' it was widely considered that slavery in Asia was somehow different, and that the trade from eastern Africa was unlike that from the Atlantic seaboard.

The Indian Ocean trade was conducted not by British or even other Europeans, but by Muslim shippers, Arab merchants who had traded with the African coast for thousands of years.

The people they purchased were not destined for the brutal, industrial-scale plantations of Brazil or the Caribbean, but for the households and cities of Persia, Arabia and Turkey.

Once incorporated into the Muslim world, these slaves became part of long-established societies, and were generally treated well. They were deeply integrated into family life and into the wider community.

In slavery times in the sugar isles, there once was an old black man, a vieux-nègre*, without the physical strength for which he was chained and brought to work.

He was a lover of silence and solitude. A mineral of motionless patience. Like an old African totem. He was said to be rugged like the coastline in the South or the bark of a more-than-millennial tree. Many said that he blazed up abruptly in a beautiful bonfire of life. Stories of slavery do not interest us much. Literature rarely holds forth on this subject in this part

---

* vieux nègre – old negro, term used in old times

of the world. It squares it's place on the world map as a tiny dot, so small that one needs a magnifying glass to see it.

However, here, in the bitter lands of sugar, we feel overwhelmed by this knot of memories that sours us with forgetting's and turns us as shrieking spectres. Whenever our speech wants to take shape, it turns toward remembrance, as if drawn to a wellspring of still-wavering waters for which we yearn with an unquenchable thirst. This man buried his maternal language of Swahili and learnt a new one. The French patois Créole. It etched the juvenile human history of the island. A history greatly influenced by variant stories, in songs in the Creole tongue, wordplay in the French and Bhojpuri tongues. He listened to his overseers and masters, toiled night and day until his sweat crusted in salt crystals under his shirt. His eyes were neither shining nor dull, but dense, like certain backwaters struck by lightning. His speech kept itself more elusive than echoes off a surfside cliff of Gris Gris.

He subjected his cabin to the manic housecleaning of the grand missié, and his survival garden, scraped out beneath the trees. So, nothing. No one knew his age. He was just a log in the ledgers. Like many boarded from Zanzibar.

He found a kind woman slave, lonely like himself and he decided to share their hut.

Thus, their togetherness brought about one daughter and one son. The daughter died after three months, out of crying and staying for long hours unfed. The mother was nursing another baby from la case Grand Missié and didn't dare to ask time to attend to her own baby. The son was sturdier and soon grew like a wild tree.

The sugar estates in the north of the country, between the flank of a volcanic mountain and thick woods – woods of dark ravines bristling with the ruins of a forgotten time, woods of symphonic streams among the mosaics of rocks, woods of singing trees, and goblins summoned in a riotous crowd by late-night storytelling into the audience-circle of fears amidst hip gyrating drums around a bonfire.

Churels probably watched in the dark for a prospective prey. Sugarcane fields surround the area, then go off to softly carpet the sea swell of humpbacked hills called mornes. Down from there, against the wall of woods, they end clumsily in a seething of muddy straw. The estates possessed one hundred and sixty-seven slaves, women and youngsters included.

Two mulatto commandeers and four sirdars oversee the daily operations.

Its memories vanished into the ashes of time. The bite of the chains. The swash of the whip. The fending cries. Sudden deaths. Starvation. Murderous fatigue. Exiles. Camps of different peoples forced to live together without the laws and moralities of the human world.

Many souls melted away there. The slaves of the first times turned themselves into writhing vines of suffering that strangled the trees and streamed over the cliffs. The slave ships of the second times have brought in indentured workers fated to bondage in the cane fields. The colonists alone manipulate the carnal masses of this heaving magma (baptizing, murdering, liberating, building, growing rich). The planters seem more like fermenting matter than like living people, and their eyes, dictating the actions of slavery, undoubtedly no longer blink in any way validated by innocence, decency, pity.

A fig for those miseries so often illustrated, let's put a name to this horror: the grandiose in-humanity that exploits human beings as an inert, indescribable density.

Gros Noir, the taciturn slave, had bleached out his life there. At the bottom of this slop, his existence has had no apparent rhyme or reason. Simply adapted to a life of obedience, the postures of servility, the cadence of planting and cane cutting, the whiff of the sugar vats, the carting of sacks to the store ships in town. He has never been scolded for anything. He has never begged anything from anyone. He answers to a ridiculous name conferred by Gros Noir. His own, the real one, grown useless, lost without him ever feeling he'd forgotten it. His genealogy, his probable lineage of papa, mama, great-grandparents, is limited to the navel sunk in his belly, like an empty coconut hole, his bearings lost forever. No one knew they bore among them a man right from the land of the cradle of humankind from Mama Africa herself.

Gros Noir has known all the stages of the sugar industry.

In his latter days, not because of failing strength but through vast experience he deals with the sugar cooking, a delicate operation he performs without seeming to deploy any expertise.

In the gleam of the boilers, his skin takes on the texture of the cast-iron buckets or rusty pipes, and at times even the coppery yellow of crystallizing sugar. His sweat dots him with the varnish of old windmill beams and gives off an odorous whiff of heated rock and mulling syrup.

In the evening after a long week, slaves gather under the huge banyan trees, exorcise their own death through rhythm and dance, tales, and fights. Certain dancers and ravanne* drummers reproach Gros Noir for his apathy. Everyone spends their nights bringing their flesh to life, with their chosen négresses. They are all thus projected, into their feverish wombs, a future renaissance, like a different version of their own existence.

Their lives are bound to the estate like the air and the earth and the sugar, more ancient than the Bois noir and tambalacoques.

Baptiste called Gros Noir Papa, as he came from his loins. The latter could, other slaves swear, purge maladies, strip away the sorrows of life, postpone the grip of death itself, whose crony he seems to be. Hemmed in by their entreaties, he places his palms on mortal pains, or puts his lips to the knotted forehead of a dying man or holds the stiffened claws of a sufferer heading off in agony to the death-land. He

---

* ravanne – a large tambourine-like instrument used in sega music of Mauritius. It is made out of goat skin called "lapo cabri" (in Mauritian Creole) which usually needs to be heated up before playing.

kisses new-borns or talks out someone seeking the nerve to run away. He learned his art from his homeland, Mama Africa, when he used to travel to Pemba island with his mama to get remedies from powerful Wgangas*.

People have seen what Gros Noir is capable of, much of which they could not explain. The taciturn slave thus gained Grand Missié's respect too. Or fear, no one would know.

---

* Wgangas – spiritual healers from Tanzania and its islands.

Chapter 17

विधवा – Widow

A dead moon hangs in the gloom of a Calcutta dawn. I glance at its ethereal presence but receive no solace. A push from rough hands and I sprawl to the cobblestones. I know I shouldn't dally, but urgency makes me bend and, with the edge of my sari, dab the fire that licks my shins. A shout, and I scramble forward, my eyes darting to a rickety gangway at the harbour's edge. A three-masted vessel sits by the shore, the sign 'Umvoti' on its side. Is this the ship? I clutch my pass and, brushing aside my tears, hurry onto the gangway. A couple of steps, and my sandal catches in a rut, tripping me sideways. One glance at the foul-smelling blackness below and the palpitation in my chest is ignored. I grip my fingers to the gangway rope and scuttle up the remainder of the plank, reaching the top, breathless, to find my path blocked by a swarthy-looking sailor. "C'mon coolie!" the man shouts, grabbing the tin ticket around my neck. "Thank you, Sahib," I murmur, my eyes fixed to the floor. Heavy breathing suggests I'm about to be hit. Instead, a parcel is thrust into my face. "Thank you, Sahib," I say, repeating myself in the hope that the man will be satisfied. Clearly, he isn't, and one look at my blood-stained sari tells me why. Head down, parcel tucked under my arm, I shuffle forward. "To the bow," the man bellows, his breath reeking of whisky. Have I gone the wrong way? Behind, a line of men, women and children board the ship. Of all ages and castes, our faces are filled, like mine with confusion. The confusion of the port. The confusion of the ship. The confusion of the life in Africa upon which we embark. A sway of the vessel, and I shriek, inching my way along the deck, before reaching a rusted ventilation shaft, where I slump and take a gulp of salt ridden air. "Move along," an Indian sounding voice says. Face down, I hold to my position. To move will only invite ridicule, even if I had the strength to do so. Thankfully, the moment passes and, with it, the spinning in my head. With reddened fingers, I trace a pattern over my parcel, before, deeming it safe to do so, prises open the ends. Inside, beneath the lining, are two saris, neatly folded, a flannel jacket and, wrapped in some brown paper below, a brass Lota. I shudder, memories of the ashram resurfacing, but at least I'll be able to wash. Bloodstains need washing. If there's water to do so, that is. I spit, rubbing the froth between my palms. It is a further humiliation, but how else am I to examine my newly acquired possessions? Sufficiently 'cleansed' (at least on the surface) my hands go to the saris. The material is soft but incites a shiver. Widows aren't permitted to wear such oranges and yellows.

Have the Sahibs no understanding of my condition? With salt stinging in my eyes, my fingers drift through the cloth, as from the greyness of the Calcutta dawn, the brilliance of the deity Usha, is imagined. Lauded in the Vedas, the oldest scriptures of Hinduism, the goddess Usha, the Hindu goddess of dawn invokes the presence of the sun god, Surya. The bringer of light and spiritual consciousness, I ward off the evil spirits of the night. A stabbing sensation envelops my chest. My parents named me Usha, after my ethereal exemplar, perhaps in wishful expectation, but I've long known that I am misnamed, that my real name is Nakti. For I am the night. Surya no longer follows my dawn awakening. Born to a life destined to be dark, I know that my smile has long since vanished, that only shadows fill my soul. Indeed, the last time I remember smiling, really smiling, was when I was six years old. Even now, all these years hence, the scene is recalled as if it were yesterday. * "Tell me the story, Baba." "Which story is that?" he says, smiling. He toys with me. Of course, he knows the story. "Baba, you know the one, about the baby girl." My indignation is only half in jest. "Ah, yes…the baby girl; let me see." He picks me up, gently, and sits me on his knee. A cool breeze wafts through the shutters, a full moon dancing on the waters of the Ganges. A jar of honey lies open on the table, its yellow liquid oozing languidly. My fingers dabble inside the jar and come out sticky, the taste of sweetness making me tingle inside.

"In a cave in the woods of Veruna there once lived a mother and a baby," he says. "This was no ordinary baby, for unbeknown to my Amma or the other people in the cave, this baby girl could fly. She had magical wings!" "I would love to be able to fly, Baba."

"Yes, that would be something, wouldn't it, my little nymph? Well, the Amma found this out one day when I went to the lake near to where they lived. I left the baby girl asleep in my crib by the shore and busied myself with my washing. I'd placed the crib too close to the water's edge.

A whale swam past, as whales tended to do at that time of the year, and a huge wave washed up onto the shore, sending the crib floating out onto the lake. The Amma cried. I thought that I'd lost my baby forever."

"Oh, Baba that is so sad."

"I know, my little nymph. Suddenly, the baby girl woke up. Something marvellous and unexpected then happened."

"What, Baba, what?" "I grew two beautiful white wings, like a heavenly nymph." "Just like me, Baba. I'm your little nymph." "Yes, Usha. Light and feathery, the wings had magical powers. As the crib sank into the dark water, the baby's wings spread wide and I flew up high into the sky, so high that I touched the sun." "Was that hot, Baba? Did it burn my hand?" "No, it was a warm and golden light. It made me feel happy." "Oh, Baba, I wish I could touch the sun like the flying baby." "You will, my little nymph, you will. Now, completely filled with joy, the magical baby floated back down again on my wide-open wings - down, down, down like a beautiful white butterfly and joined my Amma on the bank. Of course, the Amma was overjoyed. I thought that I had lost my little baby forever.

'My heavenly spirit' I cried, then gave my daughter the biggest kiss I had ever had."

"Oh, Baba, Baba, what a clever baby she is! Would you give me such a big kiss if I floated down from heaven?" "Of course, my little nymph." * A smile interrupts the gloom of the Calcutta horizon, before the thump in my chest returns. This was the last aurora. After this, I lost my smile. No longer Usha, I became Nakti, and Nakti knew that I could see only darkness, the darkness of the night. The joy of Baba's story vanishes as I remember the occasion of his departure, perhaps only a few weeks later. * I play with my doll, knowing instantly that something is wrong. What have I done to deserve such a frown? "Usha," he says. "I have something to tell you. I have to go away." "Where Baba? Where will you go?" "It's a place far away." The pounding in my chest is suffocating, as if I've succumbed to the grip of an ogre. "No, Baba, don't leave me. Why are you going?" "I have to go, but I will return, and when I do …"

"No, you can't go." Tears stream down my face. "Take me with you." "I can't, my little nymph …."

"If I was really your little nymph, you would take me." "I can't, Usha. You must stay with your Amma until I return." "No, Baba, no," I shout, clutching his leg. He prises away my fingers. For him to be so angry I must be bad. Amma holds me down. He leaves without glancing back, not once, even though I wish him to do so. It's my ugly face that he can no longer bear to look at. I sit on the porch, night after night.

Nakti, waiting for him to appear. But he never does. I'm not good enough for him to want to see me again, and however much I busy myself, thereafter, washing away my badness with my schoolwork and helping Amma around the house, he does not return. Why would he? It's the worst thing that ever happened in the world and I will not let myself forget it. His absence is a shadow that haunts me.

Even on the day of my wedding. My veil lifts, the mirror revealing a bridal sari that dazzles red sequins in flowery patterns. Beneath watery Kajal smothered eyes.

Beneath cheeks that are powdered rouge.

Beneath a crown that sits on tresses sprinkled with heady scented frangipani flowers.

Beneath a gold chain that is tied from my nose to my ear. It's the mirrored face of one older than my twelve years. A face that is Nakti's. Not mine. A face reflected that brings heaviness within. A rumble, and I glance up. An elephant strolls at the head of a procession. Astride the saddle, an Indian man wears a traditional Dhoti, his face covered by a curtain of orange marigolds. For one fleeting, glorious moment, I imagine this resplendent traveller as my handsome prince, arriving to capture my heart.

The heavy powder and petals can't disguise the greying hair and wrinkles that lie beneath nor his yellow stained protruding tooth pegs.

The reality of my marriage is no surprise. What do I have in common with a man three times my age, a man to whom I am promised by arrangement, but have met only once?

Beckoned forward, I receive from the Purohit, the sacred mantras. Head held down, I walk barefoot around the fire, making my vows in the Saptapadi*. The inevitability of my enslavement is apparent.

---

* Saptapadi – seven sacrements around the fire taken by Hindu brides and grooms during marriage

"May the night be honey-sweet," my husband vows. Night it is, for sure after that, but not honey-sweet. The lecher does not keep to his vows. I am a slave to a loveless marriage, hating my husband and hating myself more.

He dies.

Krishna has come to my rescue, or so I fleetingly imagine. "Take off your bangles," Sassuri, my mother-in-law shouts, tears of (apparent) lament streaming.

"It is your karma that has destroyed him. You have fallen. You have become inauspicious."

Although 'falling' all my life, I am shocked to discover how much so, in one day.

"What do you mean I'm inauspicious?" I shout.

"It's written in the scriptures. Have you not studied Skanda Purana?"

Fever rages like a torrent in my head. "No," I say.

"Hai Ram. The widow is more suspicious than all other inauspicious things," Sassuri says.

"At the sight of a widow, no success can be had in any undertaking. A wise man should avoid even my blessings like the poison of a snake." Sassuri words are spat, as if my mother-in-law is the snake that poisons.

I flinch, the darkness that lies within imagined, and before I can recover, Sassuri is yelling once more, this time to my sons. "Pin her down you good for nothing!"

Strong arms force me to a chair.

"Get off me," I say, trying to resist. My wrists are tied, the glint of a blade flashing.

"Don't cut me," I shout.

"Hold still." A hand catches my neck. I pull against the twine.

"I said; hold still," Sassuri says. "Or - by heaven - I will cut your throat."

I draw in air, but none arrives, my chest wheezing like an Indian shruti box. "Still, I said."

And then, the sharpness is licking my head, tresses of my shiny black hair falling like whispers, to the floor. The cutting complete, I'm handed a mirror.

"Feel the shame," the old woman says.

The consequence of my inauspiciousness is clear. Eyes of fire reflect from a newly bald head.

"What have you done?" I cry out.

"There's more," Sassuri replies. Spiteful fingers tear at my sari.

"Take your hands off me," I yell.

"Evil woman." My cry is a leopard's, caught in a trap, unable to reverse its misfortune. A net of muslin thrusts into my face.

"Put this on," Shashuri says. "You are Brahmin. Cover your guilt." Of course, thereafter the prophecy is fulfilled. How can it not be so? 'Wise men' avoid me, the white sari wrapping my shaking, inauspicious body, the lily of my youth wilting before it has even begun to flower. It is a lost youth that progresses into a lost womanhood also. Footsteps across the Umvoti deck distract me from my childhood memory. "Ugly widow," a woman of middle age mutters, scornfully. I flinch, even though the truth of the accusation is self-evident. Head bent, I keep my own company, an invisible boundary marking my separation, as the woman sits as far away from me as possible. Barbs of increasing savagery announce the arrival of others, obliged by the confines of the deck to position themselves ever closer to my impurity.

Eventually, a woman with soiled clothes (it can only be an untouchable) sits near, seemingly able to tolerate my status. The occasion brings a smile, but it is a false hope, the woman's scowl, no doubt, the ramification of a widow's corruption.

A sway of the ship, and I look to the horizon, my mind taken up by the darkest of memories: my husband's funeral; a day that will mark me forever.

Mourners line the riverbank. I stand amongst them, a white head cloth shrouding the burning rays from above.

There is no shrouding the heat of my husband's death, however. Obligated to honour the ramifications of my widowhood, I listen for his plea, that I may be re-joined with him in the afterlife, but his soul is a shadow and my heart is closed. It is the silence of death that resounds in my ears. A torch ignites the floating mass of brush.

"Sever the rope," a voice calls out. A flash of metal, and the pyre drifts from its tether, away from the bank. Suddenly, rough hands are at my shoulders. I glance up to darkened eyes. I am being manhandled into the river by Vashur, my brother-in-law! I scream, my legs kicking into a wall of darkness.

Mine is not self-immolation. Others do it for me.

From the floating pyre appears a vision, a goddess amidst the flames, beside the husband whom I have despised; the husband who has so maligned me. T
he deity smiles, but the smile is false, the vision joyless. All I see is the seethe of burning flesh, a life consumed by fire.

"No," I cried out. "I've had no life in this incarnation. How can I leave it?" A hand extends from the flames, seeming to beckon me in.

However, the palm is reversed, facing towards me, fingers together, pointing upwards. It is Baba's hand. "Don't leave.

Stay, little nymph," Baba says, his voice crackling above the flames.

Kala Pani

On the verge of fainting, something changes his intent. The deathly grip on my arms relaxes. I am thrown sideways, plunging into the choking blackness of the river's shallows.

"What are you doing?" someone shouts.

"I must burn, or I'll damn us all."

Pulled from the water, a dark face contorted, devil-possessed, flashes in front of me. It's the anger of an avenger that infuses my soul.

"Get off," I shout, swinging my fist into the old woman's midriff. I scramble up the bank, my fingers clawing at the mud and, reaching the lip of the shoreline, turn to watch the burning pyre float into deeper water, its acrid smoke drifting along the valley of my intended reincarnation.

A lurch of the ship jolts me from my fiery contemplation. I clasp the railing, my chest pounding. Would it not have been better to have burned, the way things have turned out? Shouts emanate from the front, and I rise. Several sailors crank a giant anchor from the sea floor. A rumble of engines, and the ship begins to ease away from the Calcutta dock.

Across the deck, every inch of the vessel is occupied, I and the other coolies packed like cattle in a pen, the crew running hither and thither, clambering over our 'cargo' to sail the ship.

My eyes turn to the ocean horizon and the thousands of miles that separate us from our destination of Africa.

It's a contemplation that brings chills to my veins.

We make fair passage until a few miles out to sea, the sky darkens, the wind begins to growl.

The pitch of the bow sends me scrambling across the deck.

I huddle at the side of the ventilation shaft, my heart pounding.

Crossing the Kala Pani* is taboo. I know that by crossing the sea, I risk defiling my soul and confronting the monsters of the black water. Cut off from the regenerating waters of the Ganges, my purified Hindu essence will be lost, the reincarnation cycle ended.

My thoughts jump to the Uttar Pradesh criminals, required to cross water to serve imprisonment on the islands of Andaman and Nicobar.

Like them, I will not return.

Born into sadness, I will die in sadness and now not even on my own soil. A roll of the ship, and I shriek. Extended fingers grip the iron balustrade, infidels dragging thorn briars through my insides. I lean over the side to vomit what little is left in my stomach and, eyes closed, ride the angry waves, chanting the Om, praying that Brahma will tell me what to do. My chant continues until, hoarse in the throat, I can chant no

---

* kala paani – black (Brackish) water, name given to the high seas

longer. I wait for my death, my lament that I am taken so young, having lived so little.

Finally, my strength dissolves. Whitened fingers lose our grip.

I slump to the boards, huddling without recognition, my death surely having arrived.

It's an eternity, or what may have been a moment, before the rocking eases. Watered eyes glance to a squall that has passed, the ship now making smoother progress. A surge of relief sweeps through me. The swell of the ocean continues to tie knots in my belly, but the palpitations inspired by the invisible monsters' anger is abated. It's a miracle that has allowed my prayers to be answered. Any reprieve is interrupted by an ugly looking Indian man marching along the gangway.

"Get up!" the man shouts. I jump up, my limbs twisting in pain, only to realise that the clap of thunder is directed to three women sitting on the other side of the gangway. Two of the women have risen, but the third, a woman with an air of refinement, remains seated.

"No," the woman mutters. "I am Brahmin; I'll not cook for others. Who are you to tell me otherwise?" The man's face balloons.

"I'm Ramcharit, the Sirdar. Now, get up and cook." From his pocket, he pulls a jambok, a strip of bullock's hide. The woman is struck. Several times, she only flinches as the hide hits her skin. Her eyes remain lost in emptiness. There is not much more one can lose beyond this.

"Your caste is removed," Ramcharit yells.

"You left it at the port. You won't put it on again until you come back."

Apparently, the Brahmin woman doesn't understand what he means.

"How can I discard my caste?" I say. "It's not possible!" "Go to your work, woman, before I thrash you again."

Of course, I recognise the reference. The temple in Puri, Orissa has been a pilgrimage destination for Hindus since the 11th century.

Dedicated to the prophet Jaganath, one of its four gates, the Singahdwara, or 'Lion Gate', houses an idol of Jaganath, known as Patita Pavana, which in Sanskrit means 'saviour of the downtrodden and the fallen'.

In ancient times, when untouchables were not allowed into the temple, they would pray to Patita Pavana.

Because of this, the temple has acquired a reputation for treating worshippers equally, requiring all to make and serve food together, eat from the same plate, irrespective of caste.

That evening, as the bandharis (caste of cooks) rinse the grit off the rice and prepare a meal of dhal and potatoes, I understand the meaning of Parag's words. We are together, high and low caste, obliged to sit alongside each other in line; the makeshift benches arranged in rows on the deck beside the kitchen. The meal is 'caste-less'; we eat jumbled up, the precious stones mixed with the clinker and scattered haphazardly. I sit with the others, munching my food, grateful for Patita Pavana's benevolence, although it's clear that many on the pangat have not prayed to this idol of Jaganath.

Backs turned, they inch away from me, no doubt shocked that the observance of tradition is interrupted. It's a pain endured, in spite of the ache in my belly from the sudden ingestion of food.

I find solace in prayer to the saviour of the fallen, chanting the mantra in my head, hoping that the darkness may ease. 'O most merciful one, if you are expert enough, then save me, the foremost of the fallen.'

That evening, I shiver beneath the chill of the ocean night, praying to Krishna that he may be merciful. How else will I survive the crossing? It's a sadness that takes me back to the worst of my memories, my parting from Amma.

The tyranny of my deceased husband's household has gone. I arrive at Amma's house to hammer upon the door. "Please Amma, let me in, I beg you," I shout. The silence that follows speaks to the limits of an Amma's love. My fist pounds the wooden panel once again.

"Amma, I've nowhere else to go. I'm your daughter."

A voice resonates through the grille. A voice that is cold, dispassionate.

"Go away. You're disgraced. I've had my share of bad karma. I don't want any more."

Of course, Nakti knows there's no hope of being loved again, but where else can I go?

"Mother, I've no one. I beg you; have pity," I say.

A miracle happens. A crack appears. I push on the door, assuming I am forgiven, but its opening is an enticement, entrance offered so that its refusal can be made, more forcefully. Before I can enter, the door slams shut again.

"Away," Amma shouts through the grille.

"Leave me alone." It is raging that mixes with my tears. "You would abandon your daughter? What have I done wrong?"

"Everything. You've darkness in you."

The weight of my widowhood pulls me to my knees.

Then, I'm shouting.

In a voice that is shrill, not mine. "Where is he? Where's Baba?" I have not been good enough for him to stay, but is he not the only person who can save me from my predicament? The silence from within incites a further pulse of outrage.

"Tell me!" I yell. It is through the grille that the venom of the most wretched vents, the fury of a wife's abandonment.

"Africa. You drink from the same cup. The karma is polluted. He sowed the seeds of evil and you must follow."

I gasp. Africa…all this time and I haven't known. "But Amma, you never told me…"

"Stay away!" Amma shouts through the grille. "Immolate yourself, for all our sakes!"

The damnation of a daughter is the hardest thing to bear and the devastation is absolute, yet Nakti has always known that it must be this way.

Is that not why Baba abandoned me in the first place? A chill wind blows across the Umvoti deck, but this is not the cause of my shudder.

My thoughts have progressed to the bite of a flogging. I push open the gate, fighting back my shake.

How has it come to this? Abandoned by those I thought had loved me, is life really worth living?

With tears streaming down my face, I force myself forward. The door to Shashuri's house is barely closed, when the consequences of my transgression become apparent: a fist to my midriff, the stabbing sensation rippling to my extremities.

"First, you refuse Sati and now this! You make a fool of us twice?"

Clearly not intent on being so 'lenient' at a second time of asking, Vashur, my brother-in-law, has fire in his eyes. A blow to my head sends me reeling to the wall.

"Coward," I yell. I've had enough of being treated like a criminal. My hand strikes out, catching his face, spilling the ogre backwards.

"Hai Ram, shameless witch" he shouts.

He returns with vitriol in his eyes. A blow to my stomach draws sparkles to my eyes. Arms clasped; I'm pinned to the ground.

"The whip," a voice says.

A hand muzzles my mouth. I swing my neck and sink my teeth into the flesh, biting like a rabid dog. His squeal is that of a suwar (wildboar), the grip on my arms tightening. It's the anger of furies that invests me. Legs kicking out, I struggle free.

"Get off, you pig," I shout. It's an action that is futile. Rolled over, I'm pinned down. Like cloth in a press. "Do it," a voice says. A slice, and I shriek. Then more slices, the leather bullwhip cutting my flesh. I scream. For the soreness in my back. For the throb in my belly. I scream; multiple screams at first, then whimpers as my head clouds into greyness, as numbness envelops my extremities. Then even the whimpers are no longer possible. It's the silence of nothingness that remains. I awaken with a jolt, my eyes flashing to the wooden panels of a cart, before dizziness brings the blackness once again. The next time I wake, my knees are crunched up to my belly, the burn in my back like an inferno.

"Don't move," a voice says. Through the fog is a face. Old, withered; mercifully not Shashuri's.

"Where am I?" I say.

"The ashram at Vrindavan." The room spins like a vortex. "What?"

"He brought you last night," the old woman says.

"Who?" "Your uncle. He said you'd been whipped. Stopped them from beating you. You'd have died, he said." The skin on my back is on fire.

"Died?"

"Death is for the lucky ones," the old woman says. "You must make penance for your sins, widow."

"My sins?" The old woman's face darkens. "Do you mock me? You'll take the name Dasi.

A servant of Krishna. Now pray to him like the rest of us widows. The sacred writings of Dharmashastra require it. Do we not wait to rejoin our husbands?"

"What?! I want to leave"

"Where would you go? Stay; make penance. How dare you suggest otherwise?"

The next time I wake, I'm alone, the gloom of the room interrupted by a solitary shaft of light from a window cut into the rafters. I sit up and groan, my back aching, as if prodded by hot pokers. A rattle, and a wrinkled face appears at the door, the same face as before.

"You're awake," the old woman says.

"How long?" I mutter.

"Three days and three nights. Have you the strength to rise?" I nod, although wondering if I have.

"Come; you are in time."

"For what?" My question is left unanswered. I shuffle to the door, left ajar.

Outside, steps lead to a courtyard and a gate that offers the prospect of escape.

"It's locked; for you," the old woman says, looming from the shadows. A toothless grin accompanies eyes crinkling. Head down, I follow the old woman through an arch to a shrine where a group of women sit cross-legged, chanting mantras.

Widows. Of course, the Om does not work.

By dusk my throat is dry, my soul remaining uncleansed. A cup of rice is thrust into my hand, but - my willingness for life relinquished - it slips to the ground. A new day is unwished. In the alley, I hold out my palm, mimicking the others.

What else can I do? Otherwise filled with the shame of a widow, my stomach has nothing inside it. Is this my fate? Do I, like the others, wait for the time when I may follow my husband into the field of death?

It is a void, seemingly inescapable. A void that will require a miracle.

One day, whilst begging in the alley, a man approaches me.

His smile is alluring, the sparkle in his eyes, the flash of a Golconda diamond. "Hello, I'm Vishal," he says.

Of course, I should have seen it coming; that Vishal had spent the morning walking the bazaar and was thankful to have found a candidate for his entrapment.

A coin drops into my basket.

"I see you're a widow?" he says, his eyes sparkling.

"Yes, thank you," I say, finding a smile creeping into my face.

"What's your name?" "Usha."

"Ah, like the dawn." His smile is thin.

"But is there dawn in your life, I wonder?"

"No, I'm a widow, I have only darkness."

"Oh, but I see you've not lost hope. There is a twinkle in your eyes!" "No, I think you're mistaken."

"Yes; I think you dream of escape, of riches and golden opportunity?"

If only I had seen it; the thrill of his entrapment.

Like a Venus flytrap, the stickiness of its honeyed aroma encasing its victims.

"I offer you freedom in a land of plentiful luxury," he says.

"Where is this strange land?"

"Ah, you see; you do have hope. I thought so …"

He licks his lips, the honey (I can see in hindsight) tasting sweet.

"I offer the chance of escape, a journey across the ocean, a journey to a land of wondrous possibilities."

"But where is this place?" I say, my head swimming in confusion.

"Africa. The land of plenty, the land of riches, the land of freedom."

My eyes flicker, the meaning of his smile only understood with the unfolding of time. His smile in his pocket: one more 'fly' and this month's quota met.

His smile is to his advantage: upon no limitation onto how he'll spin his enticement.

How the 'miracle' of his entrapment will allow me to join the thousands of Indians enticed into indenture and transported by the white colonists to work on the plantations in the Indian Ocean.

He smiles at himself - so wide that his mouth may have reached even to his ears if only I'd had the foresight to see it! The prospect of escape to a land other than my own, brings thrill to my core. May I yet hope for a miracle, however much tainted, to find the father who has abandoned me?

My mind drifts to the story about the baby girl that could fly. I close my eyes to Baba's smile, but when I 'look' his face is shadowed, a face different from the one once remembered. Have I forgotten his real face and invented another to replace it?

The fragmentation of my memory sends a shiver through me.

Even his absence is forgotten! Tears roll down my cheeks as I consider the void that is left in my life. I pray that I may find him in this distant land, that things may be right again, as they were before, when I was six: happy, laughing, protected. Like the baby girl that could fly.

I wonder if the gods require that I endure my inauspiciousness, the shadows that cloud my life, so that I may be reunited with him.

I fall asleep, clinging to my expectation, but my dream that night holds only darkness.

The monsters of the kala pani swallow my fragment of hope and spit it out in disgust.

How may I have thought otherwise?

My karma is bad after all. There is no time for redemption. I don't know what my sins are anyway.

Chapter 18
Pilgrimage

Bêti remembered the sickly-sweet smell of flowers turning brown in the sun, trampled offerings, scattered and rotting on the steps of forbidding temples dedicated to fantastic garishly painted gods and goddesses.

The heady and seductive scents of sandalwood and frangipani - Gulaïti! She mouthed the word almost with reverence as she breathed in a hint of the musky, ancient fragrance she remembered from the weddings she attended with her Maman. Brides and grooms wore flower garlands made of Gulaïti with thin golden threads interwoven alongside.

There was no other perfume that spoke the essence of Mauritius with as much power. She could almost feel the touch of a thin dry hand, grasping her own, as she followed behind the hurrying figure, tottering along on her little legs, her muslin skirt rustling through laneways crowded with stalls and people, whiffs of celebratory seven curries in the air. Her eyes fixed on the bright sari as it swayed ahead of her. Her mouth watered with the memory of forgotten tastes. Mango, thick and juicy, of compote with sweet and tangy tamarind, milky rice pudding on a banana leaf, a dish made as a special treat for removing the 'unmarried-ness' from brides as an early morning ritual among seven virgins.

Her mother's face rose before her, the features hazy but idealised to perfection, an image fixed forever in her mind, as no picture of her survived to tell the truth of her loveliness. She recalled the sensation of being lifted to sit on her mother's lap, the rustling of silk, the fleeting fragrance of roses rising from her clothes at her every movement, her high happy laugh.

After months of research and scouring both the island and the ancient records, Bêti chose to visit Ganga

Talao, a sacred lake in the high plateau. Pilgrims flock here during Maha Shivratri carrying decorated Bamboo structures edifying lord Shiva called Kanwars as part of their pilgrimage.

The lake in the midst of this pristine lush spot was brought to its sacred status when water from the holy river Ganga was poured into it, thus linking it metaphorically to Ganga herself.

Pilgrims take water to pour over Shiva lingas around the temples of their locality during Shivratri.

Bêti loved the peace and quiet, interspersed with bird's song and some sudden chatter from the macaques on the Jako hill where Lord Hanuman, the monkey God's shrine, overlooks the lake.

Today, it was a quiet day. The temples were deserted. No visitors, no pilgrims.

It was a stunning corner sadly covered with concrete buildings as part of lobbyists and political displays.

There was no need to spoil such natural spots in the wake of legions of fervency.

Bêti went to the shore of the lake, took off her slippers, and walked down the steps into the water. Her toes were immediately bathed in the cool water. She looked to the islet in the middle of the placid lake. She joined her palms together, closed her eyes and paid her greetings to Mother Nature, mother Ganga and everything around her. Her Maman would have been very pleased to be with her, but her spirit lives on, here or elsewhere, scattered across the elements. Pulling out a piece of coconut she picked from the offerings, she sat down to munch on its sweetness, taking in the stillness around her. She thought that nothing lives on our planet without death and decay. From this spring new life, and from this birth will come new death.

This spiral of living taught her to become a sower of seeds too, a planter of seedlings, a keeper of saplings, a part of the cycle. The forest itself is part of much larger cycles, the building of soil and migration of species and circulation of oceans. The source of clean air and pure water and good food. There is a necessary wisdom in the give-and-take of nature its quiet agreements and search for balance. There is an extraordinary generosity. Working to solve the mysteries of what made the forests tick, and how they are linked to the earth and fire and water, made each human feel connected. She watched the forest around the lake, and she listened. Her heart made louder sounds than her surroundings.

It was mid-afternoon already. Mist crept through the clusters of tropical firs, coating them with a sheen. Light-refracting droplets held entire worlds. Branches burst with emerald new growth over a fleece of jade needles. Such a marvel, the tenacity of the buds to surge with life every spring, to greet the lengthening days and warming weather with exuberance.

This is what made this land so beautiful. It looked so fresh as if it had just received a water spray to clean each branch of each leaf, making the green look so vivid. She wondered what the first indentured workers and slaves thought when they arrived. Were they as enraptured as her?

Their long treacherous voyages and the hurt of their chains would have probably numbed their senses to the virgin beauty of the landscape around them. But for now, Bêti felt invigorated and decided to carry on the peace within her home. She had better leave before the clouds got darker and heavier. They moved fast on the high plateau and a drizzle turning into a downpour, was only too frequent.

A mother is the first recollection of a baby when it comes into the world. Her scent, her touch and vision of her are what makes a child feel comforted as part of his or her cognitive abilities, in its long development. Bêti could not comprehend how an orphan who has never seen her mother or remember her face could survive. Yet they do. So was her own Maman. The human need to belong, and the personal need to struggle, to achieve conflicting ends, to find ourselves, we face disorientation, paradox, impossibility, and triumph, and all of these in the context of deep relationships, hurtful and healing, with those who make us into the people we become.

The core of who we are, struggle and surrender, integrity and equality, is expressed in our relationship with others.

Bêti could relate what it meant to be severed from their motherland in the case of the slave or indentured immigrant. Both suffered from the imbalance in the natural course of life of a human being. Trying to piece together evidence from her research to give her Maman peace, posthumously, was a quest Bêti was battling to reconcile.

The next course of action would be to further all the clues into a conclusion. Bêti thought of putting an advertisement in the local dailies. If only anyone could come forward bringing one clue to either Mohan or Maude, it would erase many long years and generations of hurt, buried in oblivion. What does she ask for? She had no words to think for this fictional ad in her head, instead she decided to make herself a cup of tea. They say a cuppa heals the toughest of problems, and the island's vanilla brew was magical. She put the kettle on and got her favourite hand painted mug. It was Portuguese, and she made sure she brought it with her to Mauritius. It was a pain to wrap it in such a way that it would absorb all types of shock during the travels and make it in one piece. The kettle hisses, spurting vigorous steam.

Bêti rushes to it and pours hot water over a 3 Dames tea bag, watching it release its tawny colour as it brews. A pleasant aroma of tea and vanilla reaches her nostrils, and it soothes her immensely.

She thinks of her childhood friend Artee who introduced this brand of tea to her by sending her a token of affection, one Winter. The taste of this long-forgotten tea from her native island made her emotional and weep when she swallowed the first mouthful. It brought back memories of her Maman and her in their home with happy moments of conviviality, sipping a cup of tea, morning and afternoon while their dogs slept by their feet.

She had been completely cut off from her island after her Maman's demise, and she had lost the taste of what a simple Mauritius brew was like. She felt like hugging Artee each time she drank this tea. But then, her affection for her had always kept their friendship unique, in ways which got lost in translation.

Bêti added some powdered milk to the dark brew squeezed as much of the tea bag as she could, where all the flavours resided.

If only this was possible, to undo the past, squeezing out all the clues and reveal the truth. She could finally speak to her mother that she has found the lost link, the unknown face of her mother's mother, grandmother, great grandmother and great grandmother.

What sense could they make of a secret kept for so many decades? How many conversations were, in retrospect, lies of omission?

If old taboos, about being the child of an interracial relationship, or the child of adoption, or being conceived via a sperm donor, were a thing of the past. Why was it that the shame surrounding these origins felt so palpable even now?

How to treat these strangers, who'd come abruptly into their lives, these strangers with whom they shared genetic material? Are these people 'family' and if not, do we need a new category to describe them?

Is it always better to know that these genetic relatives exist?

Is it always better to know the truth? Should they invite the truth over for weddings and festive dinners? Secrets, we are all discovering, have a propulsive power all of their own, and time and complicity only make them more powerful.

Once you decide to keep a secret, the secret maintains a circular logic, even when circumstances change.

Many seekers say the fact of the secret is the thing that nags at them, more than the nature of the secret itself. DNA testing has brought the past forward to the present, forcing us to grapple with decisions made long ago in different, often desperate, circumstances. It forces us to think about the people whose truths have been hushed up for decades.

Some are left with only questions, and there is no one left to ask.

In the journey that is our lives, it is what we become along the way that matters.

All that we see do and feel is what we become.
We are made of all that we have known, all that we have loved. Even all that we have lost. For as we live our lives, our lives also live us.

Bêti brings her thoughts back to the present, as she stands with her nose flattened against the iron railings, night pressing, dark and secretive with shadows.

Here and there is a golden pin-pricked flicker of light. The street outside, never quiet during the day, is now dozy with slumber. Wafts of dinner being cooked, float in the air in the neighbouring houses.

Bêti likes this moment, in the late afternoon. Each one savours that end of the day when labour comes to an end and freedom is savoured.

'A rummage in the old photos of Maman, that's what I should do' she hears herself thinking out loud. Putting thought to action, Bêti pulls out the box containing all the old photographs. Many of which were in odd sizes, depending upon the age, and some had turned sepia. She saw herself in many and wondered how she managed her long hair now that she can't even bear a centimetre more of growth from her short pixie hair style. She looked at one with her Maman in a red silk wrap-around dress, holding her hand, near the Black River Gorge. Out of the pile, a tiny one attracts her attention, she remembers it but as far as she recalls, as a child she never bothered to identify the people in this photograph. Maman used to tell her that her Matante Thérèse gave her this as part of her inheritance of furniture and other items. She said they are from your Mum. Bêti grabbed a magnifying glass and looked closely at the figures in the picture. A gentleman with a moustache and hat held close to him a beautiful woman with light hair, in front of them were two young girls. They looked like some European family from a vintage era, with a colonial villa behind them.

Bêti suddenly felt her head spin, she had to stop for a moment to gather her breath. This wasn't impossible! All that she has been looking for was right there in the drawer.

Could it be it? There was nowhere she could fathom Maman would have this photo and not know who they were … the needle in the haystack was right here, in front of her. She now needed to confirm what she thought it could be. She took a picture of the tiny photograph and tried editing it on her phone. She zoomed in on the woman's face, and something startled her. The nose and those lips! Yes, they were shadows of her Maman's looks. This is going too fast now, there are still huge gaps of two generations which are unaccounted for, like a cart in front of a bull.

The next day, she posted an ad in the dailies with the picture in clearer definition, asking for anyone who could recognise the people in the photo to get in touch with her.

"Avis de Recherche

Qui peut reconnaître cette photo de famille?

Si vous avez la moindre information, veuillez me

contacter.

Merci de me joindre sur ce numéro :242 5613"

She now had to wait. The following days became unbearable. Each hour weighed like a lifetime. Each click of the seconds hand bore a summon for hope.

Chapter 19

Rooted

In a dim bedroom an old woman opens a faded and creased book. Parchment hands opening a beloved novel and turning the yellowing pages to the first.

An old woman's hands in a bed in a dim and distant room. She knows this book by heart. Already in her mind's eye the old woman is speeding over the waves, miles and miles out to sea.

It is not where we begin, but where we are headed that matters. It is what we dream of often. Far out at sea there is the tiniest spot of something on the far horizon, something tiny and lost on a vast ocean.

It is what we dream that is the gift. It is what we dream our journey shall be that forms our very lives. The old woman reads the opening words of the novel; 'As a child she imagined that the tropics was where beauty must live.' I am an old woman now, but once it was not so.

On the sea horizon there is the form of a boat. A tiny wooden rowing boat drifting aimlessly on a formless ocean.

The old woman reads; 'She came from a land where the snow fell from the sky like powder and piled up high on her hat.'

I am wise now but once it was also not so... 'She came from a land where colours could not survive against the creeping greyness of everything that surrounded her.'

A pile of newspapers on the floor shows how she spent the last hour, and on the table were still remnants of a coffee, well drunk.

The whiff of mocha still floating in the air.

The old woman looks ahead to the open French windows over a terrace and beyond a lush green garden stood in silence.

The sky is blue with the promise of yet another beautiful day.

In the tropics, they abound with defiance to the unexpected interruption of rains.

Bêti wrote in her personal journal, a thing she took the habit of doing, since she was a child.

When she needed to recollect some inside feelings and emotions she couldn't say aloud, she would write. This was a big breakthrough in adapting to her state of being an only child. She had no one but herself, apart from her Maman, in her inner world.

« I discovered Caswell beach the first time I visited South Wales. Over the years, this small beach just outside Swansea, has become one of my favourite places to hang out.

There's nothing much to it; even some locals might agree, but it has stunning beauty. It's just a sheltered inlet between craggy cliffs, one of thousands along the coast of the area of Outstanding Natural Beauty.

It's sandy, with some parts covered with beach stones that form shaped mounds, according to the ocean's moods. Some pebbles are round, others egg-shaped. Some are perfect for skipping across the water. In the summer, the stones are warm, almost alive with the sun's energy.

In the winter, when ice droplets cling to the cliff's edge creating ethereal curtains of bluish white, the cold bites into your skin and the stones are best left alone. I learnt that covering my exotic coloured skin out of the tropics, would help not to feel them like shards assaulting mercilessly on a windy day.

Officially, you're not supposed to collect the beach stones, but somehow, over the years, at least a dozen has found their way into our home. I can't help myself, like everyone else. The beach stones are smooth and soft, sharp edges worn away by their constant tumbling in the ocean's waves, with patterns and colours unique to each. At home they lie cool and heavy, each a comfortable weight in the palm of my hand. One has a thick quartz vein running right across it. Another, round like a perfect pumpernickel loaf, is purple, tiny bands of grey circling its balanced shape. When they are wet, each one is a jewel, glowing rich and warm, but when dry, they almost fade into one another. Indistinct, their meaning is collective, rather than singular.

As a group, these stones hold the rhythm of the sea; together, they make water music: a serenade of waves rising and crashing against the shore, and then, as if in response, a clattering rush of stones spilling over each other at the water's edge. As they bump and roll against one another, they tell each other's stories, too, shaping and polishing that smoothness that I cup in my hands every summer.

Like them, too, I have discovered, shapes the story of my family, a collection of tumbling stones worn smooth by oceanic migrations, each one a fragment, together with an always moving landscape of histories, memories, longings, and dreams. I have no roots here. Just an alliance by marriage. There is nothing that binds me to this windy rock in the North Atlantic, no family history that clings to the cliffs or washes up from the seas. But it is here, among the polished stones of Caswell, that I first began to grapple with questions of origin, here that I started thinking about the meaning of home, here that I began to work through my own desires for belonging.

Home is important to Mauritians, a place central to their identity. Many can pull their family histories across this island, tracing stories that go back centuries. They can picture the places where their great grandparents lived; they walk the paths of their ancestors; they know the voices of those who have come before them. As a people, they are one with the land, deeply rooted in that place, profoundly shaped by weather, landscape, and the volatile moods of the sea.

"Where are you from?" people would ask me upon the first encounter.

I would struggle to answer.

"Most recently from Bristol" I eventually would say, and it was true. "You must have married a Welsh" they would say confidently, because they couldn't imagine any other possible reason to be here. That wasn't true. I'm a Mauritian, born and brought up on a tropical island. Someone who doesn't quite fit, whose roots haven't dug themselves into this soil or crawled along these rocks. I found out with the ocean lapping at my toes, it has brought all of this into high relief. I've spent much of my married life on the outside, looking in. I've never lived in a place that I could fully call "home."

I am rootless, my selves spreading across continents, my histories spanning cultures, globally.

Belonging is fragile, fragmented, and multiple. It is for those who are fortunate. calling it 'Home' seem impossible. I am an outsider within, someone who can take on the guise of the local, but who will never be fully recognized as one, and, perhaps more to the point, will never truly feel like one.

"Where do you belong?" I hear. "Who do you belong to?" "I'm a child of the world." An easy answer. It is true. I've lived in many places.

Yet a child of the world, is also a child without origins. A child of the world has nowhere to hang her hat. No place to call home, no place where she can ground herself. A child of the world is not uprooted, but unrooted. A chameleon constantly changing her colours, she becomes a mystery even to herself, a cipher that nobody understands.

Those of us who have moved around a lot, leave traces of ourselves in various places. Home is a collage of scattered experiences and memories. More than this, it's a mirage, something intangible and inscrutable that we can never quite touch, always just out of reach.

I've never felt like I belonged anywhere. Maybe it's because we moved so often. Maybe it's because I'm brown in a world run and staged by whites that obscures what might otherwise be seen as an apparently unambiguous ethnic heritage. Or maybe it's because, since childhood, nobody else has seemed to think I belonged either.

She had just read the small ad in the newspaper and saw the black and white print of the photograph. Her heart sank. There was no one to reach out and call when she saw it.

All of her loved ones were in their own homes away from her. This was her grandmother who was in the photograph. Who was this person? A friend? A lost relative? Or someone she was not allowed to mention. Her mother made her promise to follow in the steps of her own mother.

It was a deep family secret. Not meant to be known to any soul but herself. But the summon to the ad was far too mysterious. It had piqued her curiosity and far more beyond it.

There was a phone number in the ad, perhaps she should call? She picked the phone and dialled. She waited to hear the voice at the other end. Silence can be deafening at times.

'Allô' said someone softly. The old woman felt relieved at the tone of the female voice, although she wasn't sure what to expect at the end of the line.

'Allô, bonjour, je vous appelle au sujet de votre annonce*.'

---

* Allô, bonjour, je vous appelle au sujet de votre annonce – Hi, Good Morning, am calling regarding the advertisement.

Bêti felt her throat dry and couldn't reply for a moment. There was an awkward silence. Then she spoke.

There was no doubt that it was what Bêti was waiting to hear. She felt a tight band around her head and a frisson down her spine.

'Oui, je vous écoute, je m'appelle...' she couldn't finish her sentence when she was firmly interrupted.

'Non, c'est moi que vous allez écouter, d'où tenez vous cette photo?'

Bêti was taken aback by this sudden tone and question. She breathed in while thinking quickly how to introduce herself and answer. It was too long and complicated to sum up in a couple of sentences over the phone. After giving her name, she spoke calmly, weighing each word.

'Je sais que cela peut vous sembler incompréhensible mais il serait mieux qu'on se rencontre, je pourrais tout vous expliquer.'

There was a silence at the end of the line, then the lady said yes, and gave her a place and time for the next day. She put down the receiver with the polite 'Au revoir.'

'What had just happened?' Bêti talked to herself. She stared at the cushion she was holding on her lap, to the border with pom-poms, fiddling with them.

What now? All she could do was try to visualise the lady. What did she look like? Who was she really? Why the serious tone? Almost cold.

Well, she will find out tomorrow.

She went to the bathroom and gave her face a splash of water, she needed to cool herself down.

She looked at herself in the mirror focusing on her nose. She did inherit the pert nose from her Maman similar to the lady with the hat in the photo.

She suddenly rediscovers a feature of her face, she had never liked.

It was very much unlike a typical 'Indian' nose, she hated it, but it all shone in a new light now. Could it be what we call 'led by the nose' which will give the clue?

A breeze moves the leaves of the tall pine tree in the garden. It's tapered top sways gracefully, while at its foot a bed of Cana lilies displayed their deep scarlet flowers amongst the delicate baby pink begonias. The basalt stone borders have ferns and orchids in a tidy display of greenery. Loneliness here swoops like a sudden murmuration of sparrows filling the sky.

Floréal is nested on the highest place of the central plateau. It gets copious amounts of British like drizzles and cool air. A dead crater is the testimony of its violent volcanic origin some two hundred million years ago, but now, the place basks in complete quietness. Many upper middle-class gentrified elites and embassy staff have taken this damp corner as residences. It is far from any city hum but breathes a sophistication only understood by those of the past era.

Morning came, gentle and cool as usual. The old lady wrapped her crocheted shawl around her frail shoulders and sat down on the open veranda. She is served her morning coffee by her help, Beena, who starts the day's chores around the house.

Today, the sky feels like a happy shroud of blue. The morning sun in Floréal always seems to be on its best behaviour, never too hot and never too shy. Just right, like a soft mellow caress. Perhaps that's why many Europeans have taken to this place, when they are not of the crop of transient tourists, hurrying to have a lobster tan before going back to their lives, under gloomy grey skies.

'Madame Francine, there's a young lady who has come to see you, should I let her in?'

'Oh, she's already here, of course. Let her in, thank you.'

Francine continued sipping her coffee, taking in the restorative warm sun rays on her face.

The veranda is very lush with a display of anthuriums of pink blush, peach, white and red shades.

A huge brass pot held an exuberant fern plant and sat next were earthen pots with money plants and fox tail ferns. The lawned garden was immaculate.

'Bonjour Madame'

Francine turned to look at the figure behind her, her vision still blurred by the morning glare of the sun. A young woman with an olive complexion and bright hazel eyes was looking at her, hands clutched to a handbag.

The morning was still, the wind from the south-west soft and teasing. The sky and sea merged in the distance, blue on blue. The day was held, breathless and hovering, like a kestrel poised, wings fluttering, over the Black River gorge. It was one of those days that was too still, the lack of wind unnerving, making the morning seem as if it had drawn in on itself, gathering and collecting in a silence that should be listened to.

'Bonjour, approchez-vous ma fille' beckoned Francine to the young woman.

'Merci' and Bêti came closer.

'Asseyez-vous'

'Merci'

Bêti sat on one of the large rattan armchairs with plush calico cushions. She looked at the old woman and felt like she had lost her tongue. She could not find any words to say next, so was relieved that the old lady spoke first.

'Qui êtes vous? Et d'où tenez vous cette photo?'

After briefly introducing herself, Bêti told Francine that she was researching her mother's ancestry. And in a few minutes told her about her findings, and how her mother always had had this picture passed on to her from her Aunty, as being all, she had from her mother.

Beena, the same woman who let her in, came forward.

'Will you have some tea?'

'Yes, please. Thank you'

'Beena, tea for Madame and more coffee for me please. Bring some biscuits too.'

'Bien, Madame' replied Beena with a quick glance towards Bêti.

The latter pulled out the photo from her bag and handed it over to Francine. She had replayed this scene a hundred times in her head after the telephone call. What would be this person's reaction be when she showed the photograph?

Francine held out her frail and bony hand, where age and wrinkles had made her skin almost translucent. She had a little shake and took the photo, adjusting her glasses to take a closer look.

'Oh Mon Dieu!' Stroking the picture gently with a finger, she lifted her eyes to query Bêti. A shrug was all she got, and moist eyes. Bêti didn't realise her emotions were so visible. She was looking at the person who perhaps held the key to her Maman's past.

If only she was here …

'This is my Aunty here, my mother's sister, Bernadette. Bernadette De la Tour.' Words suspended in air. Bêti shook her head vigorously.

'De la Tour, like De la Tour in Paul et Virginie?!'

'Yes, indeed, the same.'

'I thought it was fiction. Do you mean Madame De la Tour really existed?!'

'En chair et en os, oui Mademoiselle. Ce Cher Bernardin de St Pierre.' Beena arrived with the tea and coffee. A wooden platter with a dainty porcelain teacup and saucer, milk jug and sugar pots, and a plate of biscuits.'

'Tenez, allez-y prenez votre thé, cela ne se fait pas attendre.'

Bêti was glad that this tea break provided an interlude to their conversation.

Of all things, she could not believe that one of the most famous classical literary fiction had a real figure in it.

A figure that had a direct link to her Maman's photograph, inherited from her own mother.

The vanilla laced tea was better than expected, possibly due to the heaviness of her emotions. The hot brew felt comforting, almost dislodging the lump in her throat.

After a moment of silence, sipping her own coffee, Francine beckoned Beena again. The help came back almost immediately, bringing an old book which she handed to Francine.

The latter opened it and handed it to Bêti. 'Here, have a look, you have younger eyes, you might see the details better. Alas, mine can only rely on what I remember.'

Bêti took the book and examined the hard-bound dark grey cover with golden letters on the spine.

Inside the title was repeated and the author's name at the bottom of the page;

La malédiction des Trôpiques

Bernadette De la Tour

The pages had gone yellow with brown streaks and the book had a musty smell. Time leaves smell behind. Yet no one tells you about the olfactory traces of Time.

In the first chapter, there was an engraving of a woman in a small boat with an oar in her hands.

'C'est ma tante Bernadette' said Francine. She told Bêti how her Aunty was in agony upon learning that one of her daughters had perished at sea. She drowned herself after a yearlong of bereavement, losing her husband at sea. He went to save the unfortunate passengers from a sinking ship at Île D'Ambre.

He never returned back. Maude …. she had eloped with a coolie. Committed a taboo and paid dearly for it. Those days, things were different.' Francine stopped as if she had said too much. She heaved a sigh and sipped more of her coffee.

Bêti was stunned, her cup of tea had gone cold. She put it discreetly on the coffee table.

She felt she needed to breathe some fresh air, realising she was sat outdoors.

'So, Madame, this means that maybe you are connected to my Mum's past? The lost link?'

She looked at Francine with her wide eyes trying to gulp in as much as she could of the old lady, etching each of her features in her memory.

The latter advanced her hand and touched her wrist gently. It felt cool.

'Francine, you may call me Mamie Francine, …. if you like, it looks like we are indeed connected, as you say. I know that my sister, one day in her madness, went to the beach, took a boat and went to the reef. They found the boat a few days later. It was empty. Her body was never recovered.

I found her writings. During the whole year she cried for her beautiful daughter Maude. What a loss! I read pages and pages of her love, regrets, agony and despair, many times. Then one day I decided to get them printed, and here it is.'

Francine caressed the book and looked at it lovingly as if it were a child.

"Bernadette found herself on the sea wall: the tide was out; before her the sandy plain stretched away over a kilometre. It was a long time since she had come to the Brittany coast, and she was unfamiliar with the activities in fashion there now: kites and dragon tails.

The kite: a coloured fabric stretched over a formidably tough frame, let loose into the wind; with the help of two lines, one in each hand, a person forces different directions on it, so that it climbs and drops, twists and is gone. The soft sand under her feet feels warm but it fails to climb all the way to her heart to warm it.

Her heart is with her beautiful daughter gone too early, her duty is with her husband bound to his status, her soul is trapped like a caged bird fighting for escape. Days brought her nothing but longer hours to grieve, nights didn't appease her tumultuous mind.

Bêti was at a loss, she needed breathing space to shout out her frustration and relief. She had found the answer to her long searches. She wanted to be on her own, to speak aloud to her maman.

'I will get going now, thank you for your time and for …everything. It means a lot to me. You don't know what gift you have given me today. I wished my maman was alive and had met you.'

She got up and wiped her moist eyes. Francine didn't move.

'OK then, Au revoir Mamie Francine'

'Au revoir ma chérie, will you come back to visit me?'

'Sure! Avec plaisir …' she bent down and pecked a kiss on the saggy cheek, Francine offered, while she tugged Bêti with one hand.

'Here, have this book, I want you to read it. And …. keep it'

'Oh Mamie! Merci.'

A bulbul came flying and perched itself on the edge of one of the armchairs. Its red throat contrasting sharply with the blue-black feathers of the body, it was waiting for some crumbs to be left on the coffee table.

Bêti bid goodbye to Beena and walked the long alleyway to the wide iron gate. Her heart felt sad and happy at the same time.

She looked up and saw a straw tail circling high up in the deep cerulean sky. She rubbed her nails remembering how she used to do this when she was a child.

People believed that by doing so and making a wish, it will come true. She then stopped rubbing her nails against each other.

'You already have granted me my wish, thank you!'

Out on the reef, the death of an individual, be it man or fish, offers nourishment for others; hundreds of . seas-creature profit from the demise of one.

In the solitude of decay, skin lifted from muscles, then muscles from bone, the process hastened by the oxygen-rich waters.

As ligaments and tendons part ways, pale grey bones jostle and roll on the sandy floor, in crevices, gently nudged by the swell. Here they knock against rocks and corals, each strike splintering and abrading them further against the hard substrate.

Then finally, one day, propelled by the surge of a wave and unnoticed by any living creature, all that remained of a life dissolves into seawater.

The constant actions of the sea, the ebb and flow of tides governed by the moon and the sun, pushed the remaining particles from the pool. In a rush, the last traces are pulled through and over the reef, dragged swirling into the midnight-blue drop-off.

From here they are caught and shepherded by the rich ocean currents, dispersing the remains far and wide. Some sank into the crushing depths, falling into blackness while others rose, borne out to the horizon under the bright equatorial sun.

Many months later, the waters carrying a smattering of these molecules, ushered by strong ocean currents, towards a beach, painfully bright under the sharp tropical sun.

In an inconsequential crashing of white foam, they rushed over the damp sand, until the water reached a barrier of tanned legs sitting at the tide line.
Propelled by the dying energy of the wave the water flowed through a chain of small shells, fastened together on a cord, tied around a slender brown ankle.
The water made the shells shine and glisten, turning them darker, as if they had wept at the memory of his passing.
The owner of the chain of shells, toys with the bracelet, rough fingers gently rolling the chain.

She allowed the moment of melancholy that suddenly came upon her to stay, welcoming it as an old familiar friend.
She closed her eyes and turned her head to the sun, feeling its heat on her face.

"I miss you." Tears fought their way between clenched eyelids, silver tracks in the sun.

Memories rekindled, she felt at peace.

---

* 'Bonjour, mo bien …. ki sane la ou? Mo pas pe reconet ou?' 'Mo mama ti pe vine acheter bane zaffaire ici, Devika, ou rappelle li?'* - Good morning, I am well, who are you? I can't seem to remember you.

My Mother used to come and shop here, Devika, do you remember her?

* 'Ah sa ti Madame la sa, non? Avec sari?' – Oh, the little lady in saree you mean.

'Oui, li même, mo so tifi.' – Yes, it's her, am her daughter.

'Hein ….! Ayo Bêti mo pas fine reconet toi, excuse moi, fine vine vié astere, lizier pas trop bon'* - Ah! sorry my gilr, I didn't recognise you. Blame it on age and faltering eyesight.

www.ingramcontent.com/pod-product-compliance
Lightning Source LLC
Chambersburg PA
CBHW021754190726
48290CB00005B/1264